Wanted: Dead or alive. (Alive preferred, just sayin'.)

When US Marshal Sam Dunaway comes to Kenton Valley, Texas, to prepare for a murder trial, the last person he expects to run into is his *late* wife Celine. The same woman who ran off with his life savings and supposedly died in a boardinghouse fire.

Plain Jane seamstress Selma Nelson is surely a dead ringer for Celine. Rest assured, this demure dressmaker has a secret or three. Is there a chance Sam will understand if and when she comes clean with the truth? More likely, he'll likely lock her away forever.

What a dilemma. Either Sam sets aside his principles and arrests her, or he loses the love of his life. One thing for certain, he can't deny the resurgence of passion that's fanning the smoldering embers of their former love into a roaring inferno.

Books by Marie-Nicole Ryan

Hill Country Lawmen Series
(Contemporary Western Romantic Suspense)
Hunted

Loving the Lawman Series
(Erotic Historical Western Romance)
Mastering the Marshal, 3
Pleasuring the Pinkerton, 3, formerly Taming Talia
Seducing the Sheriff, 1

Music City Heat Series
(Romantic Suspense)
Measure of a Man
Because of You, 2
Love Me if You Can, 1
Beginnings, Short Story Prequel

David and Miranda French Stories
One Too Many (Mystery/Suspense)
Love on the Run (Romantic Suspense)

FBI Guys
(Romantic Suspense)
Broken Promises, 2
Holding Her Own, 1

Stand Alone Romantic Suspense
Too Good to be True
The Man for the Job
See You in My Dreams

Holiday Themed Short Stories
Valentine's Gift, 3
Pillow Talk, 2
Mistletoe and Mario, 1

MASTERING THE MARSHAL

Loving the Lawman: 3

MARIE-NICOLE RYAN

RYANDALE PUBLISHING

This novel is a work of fiction. The names, characters, places, and incidents are products of the writer's imagination or are used fictitiously and are not to be construed as real. Any resemblance to persons, living or dead, actual events, locale or organizations is entirely coincidental.

1st print publication: March 2017, Ryandale Publishing
2nd print publication: July 2019, Ryandale Publishing

ISBN

Published in the United States of America
Library of Congress registration number: TX 8-044-118

Dedication

To author Elmore Leonard for his creation, Raylan Givens, and to actor Timothy Olyphant for bringing Raylan to life.

Chapter One

Billy Rasmussen burst into Selma's shop, skidding to a stop in front of the counter. "Miss Nelson. Miss Nelson! The marshal just rode into town."

"Billy Rasmussen, how many times do I have to remind you to close the door when you come in here?" Not that the child had any business in her dry-goods-and-sewing-notions store. Probably it was the jar of peppermint candies she kept on the counter he craved. More than probably. And refusing his bright blue eyes and dimpled cheeks simply wasn't an option. A dusty cap covered his copper curls as he danced back and forth from one foot to the other. She moved swiftly to shut the door. Dust from deeply rutted Main Street blew in with the irrepressible youngster.

"He's heading over to the sheriff's office now. That Barnes feller is going to hang for sure."

"You don't know any such thing. There hasn't been a trial yet."

Most likely the boy was right, though. A shudder shook her body at the thought of a hanging. "Why aren't you in school?" She took a cloth and wiped a rime of dust from the counter and from the top of the candy jar.

"It's recess." He gaze darted toward the sweets.

"Is that so?" she asked, tamping down her inclination to smile. "And why aren't you playing hide-and-seek with your friends instead of poking your little nose into grown folks' business?"

"They're stupid. All they wanna do is play kid games. Not me." He pointed to his chest. "I'm gonna be a lawman like Sheriff Tate or that marshal what just rode into town."

"*Who* just rode into town," she corrected, then set about straightening the packages containing needles and pins until they were aligned just so. Billy's little mouth turned downward and his narrow shoulders sagged as she delayed giving him his treat. He glanced toward the door, so she gave in. "I don't suppose you'd like a piece of peppermint this fine morning?"

The boy's eyes lit with anticipation as he nodded. "Yes, ma'am, I surely would." He held out his somewhat grimy hand, and she dropped the sweet into his open palm. "Thanks, Miss Nelson." He popped the mint into his mouth.

"Now, go on. I don't want your teacher coming down here looking for you."

With a gleeful grin, he nodded, dashed outside, and ran down the street. Her brief interlude with Billy was a game they played almost daily. Poor child. Reckon he'd had few enough treats in his young life. His father was a part-time drunk, but the boy had a hardworking and loving mother. Somehow the woman managed to keep Billy and his four younger brothers from starvation's door by taking in washing and ironing. The boy's buoyant spirit was a miracle, and Selma had no doubt he'd make something of himself. Maybe he really would be a lawman.

If the marshal had arrived, then the judge wouldn't be far behind. The trial would take place soon. The killer of the sheriff's first wife and unborn child would face a court's justice, swift and true. The residents of Kenton Valley had long memories.

The incident had taken place right after Selma came to town. She'd been terrified when a gang of bank robbers had gunned down Sheriff Tate's young wife. What kind of town had Selma chosen to live in anyway? The unfortunate woman lingered several days and then died along with her baby. The entire town mourned and demanded justice. When two years later the sheriff found love and married again, Selma couldn't have been more pleased. She'd even helped make his new wife's wedding dress. Starling Tate was now eight months along and Selma's best friend.

She glanced down at the timepiece on her bodice. Matter of fact, she was due at the sheriff's spread right now. Past due.

US Marshal Sam Dunaway tied his horse to the hitching post in front of the sheriff's office and surveyed the small town of Kenton Valley. Typical of most small Texas towns, it had a church, a general store, dry goods, and two saloons. Down at the far end of the street was a school, where he heard the excited shouts of children playing some game or other.

He brushed the fine yellow dust from his oilskin duster and was ready to step onto the walk when a scrawny, redheaded boy ran up.

"Marshal! Are ya a-going to hang that feller what shot the sheriff's missus?"

He gave the boy his sternest expression. "Not without a trial first."

"He's guilty. Ever'body says so. I wanna see him

swing."

So young and so bloodthirsty. Sam shook his head. "I suspect your mama will keep you home that day. If you were mine, I would."

The boy shifted from one foot to the other. "Dang it. Hey, I'm gonna be a lawman when
I grow up."

"That's mighty fine, kid. Say, what's your name?"

The kid puffed out his chest. "William Robert Rasmussen, but folks call me Billy."

"Well, Billy, being a lawman is a tough job. Need to be smart—"

"And fast with a gun." The kid did an imaginary quick draw.

"Being smart's more important." Sam hunkered down to the boy's level. "How come you aren't in school?"

Billy screwed his face into a frown. "School's stupid."

"Not so. If you want to be a lawman, you gotta go to school. That's all there is to it."

"Really?" His eyes widened in surprise.

"Really. Now go on. Git."

Shaking his head, Sam stood and watched until he was sure the boy had reached the end of the street. Damnation. What was it with kids today? In a hell of a hurry to grow up, when these were the best times of their lives.

He opened the door to the sheriff's office and nodded. "Sheriff Cordero Tate?"

The sheriff nodded. "Cord'll do." The sheriff was tall and broad shouldered and showed no signs of his prior tragedy. He rose and offered his hand.

Sam took it. "I'd like to see the prisoner and how he's housed."

Tate stood and opened the door leading off the main room. It led to a cellblock, containing two cells. Only one was occupied. Barnes was stretched out, apparently asleep on the bunk-as if in a few days he wouldn't be sleeping forever.

Sam turned and walked back to the outer office. "Appears you have a sturdy enough jail. Any chance the rest of his gang might try and break him out?"

"I've got two trustworthy deputies. Besides"-the sheriff shook his head-"the gang's ringleader was killed last summer. The rest of 'em splintered after that. 'Course, you never know." He shrugged. "Catching Barnes here was more of an accident than anything. He couldn't resist visiting his sick mama. Thought he might show up, so we took turns keeping an eye on the Barnes homestead."

"Smart thinking. If I'm not mistaken, you're the one who killed the ringleader, Tyler?" Not to mention the sheriff's new wife was Tyler's half-sister. Wonder that didn't complicate things.

"That's right." Tate sat, gesturing for Sam to pull up a chair.

A man of few words. Good. Removing his Stetson, Sam hooked the toe of his boot around a chair leg, dragged it over and straddled it. Now they could get down to the business of the trial. "I need a place to hold the trial. Any suggestions?"

"Haven't had much call for trials till now. There's the school or the church or the saloon."

"Good. I'll check 'em out. Prefer a neutral ground over the saloon. Any chance we'll find twelve sober men come trial time?

Tate shrugged. "If you'd rather move the trial to a

bigger town, it won't hurt my feelings none."

Sam shook his head. "I'm here to see he gets one. Don't care if it's fair or not. That's up to the judge, not me." He stood and settled the Stetson on his head. I'll head over to the church, then to the school. Let you know which one I decide."

The sheriff nodded. "Any word on when the judge will get here?"

"Few days. He's presiding over a trial in Llano." Sam headed to the door, then stopped. "The livery?"

"Livery stables are behind the boarding house at the north end of town. Miz Foley oughta be able to fix you up while you're here." Tate jerked his head in the direction of the cells. "She provides meals for the prisoner, and she's a damn fine cook."

Sam touched the brim of his hat, nodding his appreciation.

Outside, he untied and mounted his horse, then headed north, passing the general store and dry goods. He glimpsed the tall, slender figure of a woman standing in the window of the dry goods store, a sudden apparition that had him twisting around in his saddle to get a better look. But his horse had other ideas and kept heading north.

Damn. She looked familiar, so familiar his heart sped up and his mouth went dry as sand. Just the memory of their loving stiffened his prick. But it couldn't be Celine. His wife had burned to death in a boardinghouse fire near-on three years ago.

When the news of her death had finally reached him, he'd still been too angry to grieve. She never would've died if she'd stayed home where she belonged instead of running off with his life savings. Served the bitch right—that was what he'd thought at the time.

But now... If this woman really was Celine and not someone who was her spitting image, what he wouldn't give to bed his wife one last time before he locked up the thieving bitch.

Chapter Two

Unable to believe the truth her eyes plainly told her, Selma stared at the tall, retreating figure, her hands trembling. The US marshal Billy had been so excited about was none other than Sam Dunaway, her husband from another life. Where she'd had another name.

When he'd twisted around in the saddle for another look, she'd gasped and jumped back from the window. Heavens. He'd seen her.

She raced back to the sewing room and sat, trying to catch her breath. When had he left the Rangers? What should she do? Should she run or stay and face him? She'd always known this day might come...sooner or later or maybe never. Of the three choices, she preferred never.

This time, running wasn't an option. She had too much invested in the store and in her new life. No, it was Sam's money she'd used to set up her business. She owed him. In fact, she'd almost saved enough to pay him back. But he wouldn't be satisfied with mere money. He'd want to punish her. Hell, he might even arrest her. She'd stolen his savings, run off, assumed the life of the real Selma Nelson, who really died in that boardinghouse fire, and allowed him to believe her dead.

Guess she deserved whatever punishment he deemed fit. Somehow she'd managed to bury the memories of the vibrant man she'd married for love, instead condemning herself to the life of a dried-up spinster dressmaker.

But seeing him ride past, so tall and virile in the saddle, weakened her knees, not to mention her resolve. Even now, memories of their blissful nights together surged to the fore, leaving her hungering for more of Sam's tender, sweet loving.

Dear God, what was she to do? What manner of woman would do the things she'd done without an explanation or warning?

A desperate one.

But no explanation, however reasonable, would matter. Sam Dunaway believed in telling the truth and abiding by the law. Believing everything was either black or white might be a necessity for a lawman. But he would never, ever come close to understanding the reasons behind her actions, much less forgive her.

Heaven help her. She still loved him as much as the day they married. And how had she repaid him after he'd saved her life what now seemed a lifetime ago?

With abandonment. With theft. And with the ultimate lie of her death.

Surely he hadn't recognized her. As long as she kept to herself and didn't attract attention, he would be gone as soon as the trial concluded. Maybe she should close the shop for a week.

No, she had commitments. There was the layette to complete for the sheriff's baby. And those three dresses to finish. The Grange spring dance was only two weeks away.

How could she disappoint the three young women who hoped to capture the eye of new beaus?

Truth was, she couldn't. Her livelihood depended on her finishing those frocks, but completing the layette was a favor for her dearest friend.

While it wasn't likely the marshal would interest himself in dry goods or sewing notions, he would most assuredly stay at the town's only boardinghouse—the very one where she lived.

Her mind whirled with possibilities. She could come and go using the back stairs. That way her chances of running into him would be minimal. Meals would be another matter. Perhaps she could feign a minor indisposition and ask Mrs. Foley to bring her meals to Selma's room, instead of eating with the rest of the boarders.

She rose, rushed to the door, locked it, and flipped the sign to CLOSED. Her heart still in her throat, she grabbed a bonnet and her large sewing basket. It was already stocked with the folded, soft cotton fabrics she and Star would use for the unborn babe's layette.

Did she have everything she needed? After a second's consideration, she grabbed the six-shooter she kept under the store counter and added it to the sewing basket. Best be prepared for anything.

Now, more importantly, could she get out of town without being seen? She might just make it if she hurried. She could take the back alley to the livery for her horse and buggy while Sam was occupied with Mrs. Foley.

Breathless by the time she reached the livery stables,

Selma slipped inside, grateful for the shadows the building provided. At least Sam couldn't see her. She set down her sewing basket.

"Miz Nelson, wasn't expecting you." A wide grin creased the liveryman's grizzled cheeks. "You be aiming to take a ride this fine morning?"

"Indeed I do, Mr. Foley, and I'm in a bit of a hurry."

"I'll git right on it. Your Molly be in a fine fettle. I expect she'll enjoy the exercise."

She motioned toward the sewing basket. "I'll need the buggy too. I'm headed out to Mrs. Tate's. Might be gone a day or two. I'd appreciate it if you'll tell Mrs. Foley I won't be back for dinner? I wouldn't want her to worry."

Or have a search party mounted when she didn't return before dark.

"Sure thing." Still smiling, Mr. Foley nodded and set about hitching the mare to the buggy. Everyone knew the sheriff's wife was with child and due in a month.

Just hurry. Sam would doubtless use the livery to stable his horse while in town. If she could just get out of town before he caught sight of her again...

"All ready," Mr. Foley said, patting the bay mare's haunch.

Selma nodded and climbed into the buggy. The liveryman handed up her basket. "Thank you," she said, then grasped the reins. "Walk on."

The mare walked forward at a leisurely pace.

Aiming to take the back way and head south, she pulled on the left rein.

A commotion at the back door. Gracious. It was too late. Mrs. Foley stood at the door, pointing Sam toward the stable. Nodding, he swept his gaze over the yard, then halted when he saw Selma. His chin dropped, but he recovered. His handsome face grew hard as if carved from the limestone hills that lined either side of Kenton Valley.

Good Lord, she had to get out of town. She'd tarried a minute too long. Trembling under his furious, hot gaze, she flicked her wrists, whipping the reins lightly. "G'dap!"

The mare moved forward in a nice trot. At least she had a slight advantage. She knew where she was going. And Sam didn't. But if he was any kind of lawman, and he most certainly was *that* kind of lawman, it wouldn't take him long to find out.

Risking a quick glance over her shoulder, she saw Sam bound down the steps, then race around the side of the boardinghouse for the street. Going for his horse, no doubt.

"H'yah!" With each slap of the reins, Molly picked up the pace until she was almost flying down the narrow alleyway. A lone hound barked as Selma aimed the horse and buggy past the church. If she could just get around the bend before Sam made it to his horse, she'd be out of sight. He'd have to stop and ask questions, and that would slow him down.

No, damn it. All he'd have to do was follow the cloud of yellow dust she left in her wake. Her mare seemed to enjoy the headlong rush out of town and kept up a steady gallop. If, by some miracle, Sam didn't catch up with them, she'd let Molly slow down a bit. But she wouldn't feel safe until she reached the haven of the sheriff's ranch.

With Sam's arrival, it was difficult to know who she was anymore. No doubt he would remind her, right before he arrested her. She shouldn't have bolted. Now that realization had come a little late. Besides, her panicking was a dead giveaway. Maybe she should've held her ground and pretended she didn't know him.

But how? Sam was no man's—nor woman's—fool. He didn't bluff easily, and there was no denying her reaction to seeing him again.

Sam, the love of her life—her only love thus far. So tall, in fact, she barely reached his shoulder, and she was taller than most women. And handsome, with brown eyes the color of whiskey, and dark brown hair reaching his collar. His features were as regular as if drawn by an artist. And in bed, a powerful lover, but tender, giving her pleasure beyond imagining. Yet along with those good qualities, he was exacting, a man as hard on himself as others. And he'd never forgive her.

Never.

The sight of Celine, alive and well, froze Sam to the spot. His knees weakened and his gut churned. It was his wife all right. Damn the woman to hell. She'd made a feeble attempt at changing her appearance. She'd drawn her light honey-brown hair back in a tight, ugly knot and donned a drab dress she never would've worn during their year-long marriage. But seeing her gray eyes fixed on him sealed the deal. That and the panicked expression on her face as she flew out of town like a bat outta hell.

He'd catch her. And, no doubt about it, he'd have his due.

He started to run for his horse, but stopped. "Mr. Foley!" he shouted. "Where was she going?"

Planting his feet wider apart, the liveryman set his hands on his hips and glared. "What business be it of yours where Miz Nelson be going?"

So she was calling herself Nelson now. Sam squared his shoulders and loomed over the older man. "I'm the US marshal for these parts, and if l say she's my business, then you can damn well take my word for it. *Where* was she headed?"

Foley shrugged. "Don't rightly know. Reckon she be back soon enough. Likely you be seeing her at supper."

Foley's defiant stance and shifty gaze told Sam the man was lying. "Better be telling me truth, Foley, or I'll have your hide," he said with a growl. He stepped back, remembering the Foleys had the only boardinghouse and livery stable in town.

"Miss Nelson—she been in town long?"

"Goin' on three years or so," the liveryman admitted through clenched teeth. "Dressmaker. Runs the dry goods. *Nice lady.* Quiet. *No* trouble. Don't need none from *you* neither," Foley finished with an emphatic nod.

Yeah, Celine was a charmer all right. Clear to see she'd already worked her womanly wiles on Foley just like she'd used them on Sam four years ago. Dammit. Why couldn't he have looked the other way when part of the Tyler gang set upon that stage coach and let the road agents have her? His life would've been much simpler then.

But no lawman worth drawing breath looked the other way, not when folks' lives and property were at stake.

"You're sure she'll be back this evening?"

"Reckon so. Eats supper every night." Foley dragged the toe of his boot in the dust, forming a crooked line.

Sam dipped his head in a curt nod. Foley had drawn his line in the sand, so to speak.

"She'd better. Or I'll know the reason why not."

"Yeah." Foley nodded back, then spit tobacco juice

from the corner of his mouth. It landed wide, missing the toe of Sam's boot by a couple of inches.

Sam frowned, then settled his Stetson on his head. "My horse is tied up in front of the boardinghouse. I'll be here until after the trial is over. He needs—"

"I'll see to 'im," Foley interrupted, then took off at a somewhat unsteady jog on his severely bowed legs.

In spite of a powerful inclination to chase after his thieving bitch of a wife, he still had business in town to attend to. Judge Harley Riordan from the Fourth Circuit Court would be here soon and expect Sam to have the place for trial set up and ready to commence swearing in jurors. From what he'd read about the case, it shouldn't take more than a day or two to find Arvil Barnes guilty of murder.

Once the matter of the hanging was settled, he'd see to his wife. Even if she didn't show up for her supper this evening, he'd find her, just as he'd run across her this time without so much as trying. Once he set his mind to it, nothing could keep him from finding her again.

Was it a case of revenge? No. She'd stolen more than their nest egg. First, she'd stolen his heart and then all his dreams of a family. Instead of a haven from the ugliness he saw every day, she'd become a part of it, a no-good, damned thief.

And yet, a part of him was glad she wasn't the charred remains he'd seen after the fire in Amarillo. But that raised another question or two—was Celine responsible for the fire and the death of the woman whose life she'd apparently stolen? Was she a murderer as well as a thief?

As her buggy topped the hill, Selma--would she ever

think of herself as Celine again?—twisted around and peered through the cloud of trail dust to see if she were being followed.

Nothing.

She couldn't help but let out a deep sigh of relief. But why wasn't he following her? That didn't make sense. Maybe he'd stopped to question Mr. Foley. Why hadn't she kept her mouth shut about where she was going? Maybe the liveryman would keep that bit of information to himself. She should've known she might run into Sam sometime. Texas was a big state, but apparently not big enough.

She reined Molly in a bit but kept her to a steady trot. The April sun shone brightly, and in the distance, she could hear birds chirping, along with the droning buzz of insects. To her right, bluebonnets grew in a thick carpet fit enough for royal feet to tread upon. On her left, a stand of Texas live oak spread from the road to the base of a limestone outcrop.

The sun beat down on the roof of the buggy, causing perspiration to bead on the back on her neck. She bent down and retrieved her bonnet from the sewing basket and fanned her cheeks. Damn heat. This was April. Where were the cool spring breezes she associated with her favorite season? If it was already this warm in April, how hot would July and August be?

And maybe it wasn't the weather at all. Maybe it was seeing Sam again. No point in denying his effect on her. Heart racing. Ragged breaths. Limbs weaker than a newborn kitten's.

Forget about him.

As if she could. Even now, the tender touch of his

callused hands and the sweet joy of his kisses lingered in her memory and on her skin. The light stubble on his cheeks and chin teasing and grazing her inner thighs...

God. How she wanted him. Needed him. And yes, still loved him.

Why, oh why had she run out on him? Why couldn't she have stood up to Antoine Thibodaux, who at one time had been the lieutenant governor of Louisiana, and told him to do his worst? No, that action would've created havoc beyond imagining. Thibodaux had been one of her father's friends and had known all about her mother's house of ill repute. He'd even attempted to purchase her virginity when she'd been a mere slip of a girl.

She should've trusted in Sam's love and strength. But he was gone so much with the Rangers, and their love was so new. When had he become a US marshal anyway?

Too late for regrets now. This time she'd have to stand up to Sam himself, and that scared her even more than facing Thibodaux back in Abilene.

The buggy topped the last hill. She smiled and let out a sigh of relief. Finally, the sheriff's ranch was in view. She drove across the bridge of a dry creek bed that followed along one side of the Tate ranch. A scattering of cottonwoods and willows grew along the bank. With normal spring rains, the arroyo would turn into a small river, but the Hill Country was already in the midst of a drought.

The whitewashed ranch house was two stories, the second story under a peaked roof. A covered porch ran across the front with two rocking chairs set side by side. More than likely, Starr and Cord spent many an evening in the cool shade while they planned their future and talked about the baby to come.

Regret rocked through Selma. She could've had such a life, if only...

Coward. And thief. And, being a no-good thief, she deserved the arid life she'd chosen as a spinster dressmaker.

Chapter Three

After checking out the saloon—too dirty—and the church—too small—Sam decided the school was the best place to hold the trial. Took some bargaining with Nathan MacDonald, the schoolteacher, but Sam convinced the young teacher the trial should be over in two days if not one. Depending on when the judge arrived, it was even possible the trial could be held over the week's end and wouldn't disturb the children's lessons at all.

Sam left the school and started the dusty walk back to the sheriff's office. The sun was high in the sky when he found himself passing the sheriff's office. He crossed the street and stood in front of the window where he'd first spied Celine. Over the door, the sign read DRY GOODS AND SEWING NOTIONS, S. NELSON, PROP. A smaller sign in the window's lower corner offered DRESSMAKING SERVICES. According to the small sign on the door, the shop was closed...for now, anyway.

So she'd stolen his money and set herself up as a dressmaker. It figured, since she'd proven handy enough with a needle during their marriage. He'd always appreciated how lovely she was and how she could turn a plain piece of fabric into a dress that flattered her curvy figure. She hadn't just sewn for herself either. She'd made him everyday shirts and even a fine wool suit for Sundays.

He peered through the window. Inside, the counters were neat and orderly. Bolts of material were lined up like soldiers across one side of the shop. A door occupied the back wall midway. Presumably, she did her sewing in the back room.

No doubt about it. She'd made a nice life for herself with his hard-earned life savings. Dammit! He shook his head. He would've given her the world if she'd asked for it. Why'd she have to run off in the first place?

She'd never loved him. No. She'd suckered him. That was all there was to it. And no one made Sam look like a fool twice.

No man. And certainly no woman.

Again, Sam crossed the street and stepped onto the boardwalk in front of the sheriff's office. Pausing long enough to knock the dust off his boots, he opened the door and entered.

Tate glanced up from his newspaper. "Decide on a location?"

"School," Sam said with a nod. "MacDonald was none too happy, but he came around to my way of thinking."

"Did he now?" Tate gave a good-natured smile. "Get your lodgings and horse taken care of?"

"I did." Sam hesitated, then said, "When I rode into town, I recognized someone—or at least someone I thought

I knew."

The sheriff's eyes widened. "Really?" He folded his newspaper in half and laid it down.

Sam swallowed the stubborn knot in his throat. "Woman owns the dry goods, calling herself Nelson."

"Selma?" Tate's brows drew together in a frown. "For a minute there, I thought you meant you'd spotted a bank robber or maybe a road agent."

"I do."

"Must be someone who resembles her." Tate shook his head. "My wife and I have known Miss Nelson ever since she moved here and opened her shop."

Pulling up a chair, Sam sat, straddling it, his arms propped on the back. "What d'ya know about her? Where'd she come from?" Might as well learn what he could from the local law. Like as not, Mrs. Foley wouldn't be any more forthcoming than her husband.

"What do I know about her?" Tate let out a bark of a laugh. "What I *know* is she's more'n likely at my ranch, right now."

"What's her business at your ranch?" Sam pulled the chair out and stood, ready to chase after the bitch.

"Hold on." The sheriff got to his feet and moved toward the door, blocking Sam. "My wife and I—we're having a baby in another month or so, and I don't want anything upsetting her. Star's counting on Miss Nelson helping with the baby clothes. I assure you my wife's in no danger from the local seamstress." Tate eyeballed Sam as if he were loco.

Hands fisted and down at his sides, Sam jerked his head toward the door. "I'll find out soon enough.

Just point me toward your spread."

The sheriff held up a delaying hand. "Instead, come with me for supper. Meet Miss Nelson. I assure you, she's a fine, upstanding citizen. Has been ever since she came to town. You've confused her with someone else. You'll see your error soon enough."

No sense in upsetting the sheriff and his expectant wife or blaming him for what was an honest mistake. Tate wasn't the first man taken in by a pair of innocent dove-gray eyes. Once upon a time, Sam himself had been gullible enough to trust Celine. But that day was long gone.

"I'll do just that," he said with a nod, willing his fists to relax. "Thank you for the invite." Sooner or later, an outlaw's luck always ran out. And Celine was about to learn she couldn't escape the long arm of the law—especially his.

"No rush, then?" Tate said with a raised brow. "My deputies will be here later to guard the prisoner." Pleased as punch by the way events had unfolded, Sam nodded, unable to hold back a slight smile. He had the bitch right where he wanted her, and this time there wasn't a chance in hell she'd get away.

Selma hopped from the buggy, then looped a lead rein around the hitching post. Taking a moment to catch her breath, she shook the trail dust from her skirts. She'd just turned to lift her sewing basket from the buggy floor when she heard the screen door open, the bottom scraping across the wood porch.

"Selma!" A smiling and very pregnant Starlight Tate stood in the doorway, her eyes glittering with excitement. "I'm so glad you're finally here. Come on in. I have a pot of coffee on the stove. We can sit a spell before we start on the baby's things. Tell me the news. What's going on in town? Cord never tells me anything interesting."

Selma hefted the large basket and stepped onto the porch. "Coffee sounds wonderful."

Still there was a very real need to get her horse and buggy out of sight. What if Sam managed to follow her after all? "I'd like to take care of Molly and the buggy."

"Don't give it a second thought. The foreman will take care of her and the buggy too." A short, bandy-legged man ambled around the corner of the house. "Tom," Star said, "see to Miss Nelson's horse and buggy."

He nodded and gave a quick tip of his hat. Selma thanked him as the foreman loosened the reins. He hopped into the buggy and drove behind the house. Whew. Out of sight.

Star enveloped Selma in a big hug. "You're lucky you inherited that fine buggy from your uncle. I'm sure it rides much better than our buckboard."

She returned the hug, wishing she had the nerve to tell her only friend about her past life and sins. "Yes, it was nice of him to think of me." Truth be told, the buggy had been a bequest from her wealthy father. She'd only met him twice, and he'd never acknowledged her publicly. Fortunately, he'd been generous enough to educate her far beyond what a girl child born in a high-class New Orleans bordello could've ever expected. And if her mother hadn't been the madam, Selma (then Celine) would've likely ended up working in the world's oldest profession.

The two women walked arm in arm inside the ranch house. "You've created a very comfortable home," Selma said with a smile. Frilly white curtains hung at the windows. To one side of the room was a sitting area with a settee, two side chairs and an oak rocker. No doubt the rocker would see plenty of use in the months to come. At the opposite end was a stone fireplace. Star had placed a round oak table with dinner already set for three. Selma could imagine what wonderfully cozy meals Star and her lawman husband must share while they waited for the birth of their baby.

Indeed, if she admitted the truth, she was a trifle envious-not of the house or the furnishings. No, it was the life and love the couple shared. Something she would never know again.

Quickly, she buried the pang of regret shooting through her. Because of his duties with the Texas Rangers, Sam had spent many nights away from home chasing outlaws in the far reaches of the state. His absence had made the times they had together all the more memorable and precious.

The aroma of freshly brewed coffee and the open doorway beckoned Selma to the sunny kitchen that ran across the back of the house.

Rubbing the small of her back, Star waddled over to the cookstove. "I love mornings in this kitchen. Cord built a wonderful home for Annie. Sometimes I don't think I deserve the happiness that should've been hers." Her words ended in a gulp.

Selma rushed over to Star and placed her hand on her friend's shoulder. "You mustn't think like that. You weren't responsible for her death or her baby's."

"I know, but sometimes I'm afraid we're too happy. I'm afraid we're tempting fate and that something will happen to the baby or me. Another loss would kill Cord."

Selma took the coffeepot from Star's hands. "Here, you sit." She nodded toward a chair.

"I'll pour the coffee. You're going to be fine. You're going to have a healthy baby. And it will make up for all of Cord's unhappiness."

"But I can't help but think about it. Especially now—what with the trial—it brings it all back. Sometimes I catch him watching me with worry in his eyes. He denies it, but I know he's afraid something will go wrong."

"His worrying is only natural. He loves you. Any fool can see that." Selma pulled two cups from the cupboard. "What arrangements have you made for the lying-in?"

"Cord has persuaded a young doctor from Austin to set up practice in Kenton Valley. He should be here any day now. Can you believe that husband of mine? Said he wasn't taking any chances with depending on a midwife to deliver this baby. You know his wife lingered for nearly two days after she was shot." Star shivered. "I can't imagine how she suffered. All that pain, and knowing that she and her baby were dying."

"I remember. I hadn't been in the Valley very long when it happened." Selma poured a cup and handed it to her friend. Star took a quick sip.

Selma poured another cup. "It was a tragedy for sure. It wasn't your fault, and there's nothing you could've done about what happened. But when you and Cord married, it was a new life for both of you. As tempting as it is, you shouldn't dwell on the past. The way I see it you two have the makings of a wonderful life. Don't spoil it."

"I know you're right. I guess worrying goes along with having a baby." Star chewed her bottom lip, then asked, "Do you ever regret not marrying and having children?"

Startled by the question, Selma sucked in a quick breath. The need to tell someone her secrets was overwhelming. Star was a dear friend, but the possibility of seeing dismay and disapproval in her friend's eyes stopped her.

Perhaps, a half-truth would suffice. Or a quarter. "There was someone...once."

Interest glowed in Star's gaze as she leaned forward-or tried to, since her belly was in the way. "Really? I don't mean to pry, but you never talk about yourself"

"I was on a stagecoach on the way to Abilene. We were almost there when the stage was attacked by two road agents."

"How exciting."

"Exciting doesn't begin to describe it. I was terrified. They already had us out of the coach, stripped us of our valuables, not to mention a rich payroll headed for the Abilene bank. One of them had other ideas, and he dragged me off behind an outcrop." She couldn't help but tremble at the memory. "All of a sudden, there was the sound of horse hoof beats and gunfire. The other robber hightailed it out of there, and I screamed. A Texas Ranger heard my cries for help, leapt off his horse, and attacked the second miscreant. Once my rescuer had him under control, he turned his attention to me.

"I was a mess. My hat was crumpled in the dust. I was covered in dirt, and my sleeve was ripped, but when I gazed into his warm brown eyes, none of that mattered. He picked me up in his arms and carried me back to the stagecoach. I'd never met a man so handsome and gallant before, and certainly none since."

"What a romantic beginning, but what happened? Did he just go on his merry way and never look back?"

If only he had.

Selma shook her head. "Not exactly. We courted a while, but he was always leaving town for long periods of time—on Ranger business, mind you—but it soon became apparent he wasn't the sticking-around kind." What was another lie on top of all the ones she'd already told.

"I'm so sorry." Star frowned. "But how did you end up in Kenton Valley?"

How indeed?

"That's an even longer story." Standing, Selma drained her cup and set it on the table. "We need to get busy on that layette. We can't have your first child being born without anything to wrap him or her in."

"You're right." The redhead stood clumsily and rubbed her back. "I'll be so glad when this baby comes. I know I'll never fit into my clothes again. You'll probably have to make me a whole new wardrobe," she said with a laugh.

"I'd be delighted to sew you a new wardrobe." If Sam didn't find her and slap her in jail first. "But you'll be surprised how quickly you'll get back into your dresses."

"Really?" Star's expression brightened, then was replaced by one of concern. Her hand went from her back to her lower belly. "Ow!"

"Is the baby coming?" Selma asked, more than a little alarmed. Not yet, surely.

Star smiled and shook her head. "Just a twinge...really. I have them now and again. Don't worry. This baby's still a month away from showing its little face."

"Good, because I'll have you know that I know absolutely nothing about birthing babies." Not exactly true. While hiding behind a closet door, she'd watched one of her mother's whores as her baby was delivered. Suppressing a shudder, Selma took her friend's hand and led her to the rocking chair. "Make yourself comfortable. We'll get busy and finish these baby things."

Chapter Four

The unforgiving Texas sun beat down. Sam removed his Stetson and used his bandanna to mop beads of sweat from his brow. He'd spent the majority of the afternoon on foot, checking out the town. One main street led through the center. If any of the prisoner's remaining gang had intentions of staging a breakout, they'd have to ride into town either from the northeast or from the southwest.

But he didn't expect they'd have the balls. More'n likely they'd sneak in under cover of night, then lie in wait, ready to ambush when Barnes was moved for trial. Sam had spied several vantage points where a couple of armed men could inflict serious damage. One such point was the high façade of the dry goods store. Between that spot, the general store next door, and the sheriff's office opposite, they made a perfect shooting gallery.

If Sam were a robber and of a mind to stage a jailbreak, he'd position two riflemen behind those false fronts and have two more of his cronies waiting in the back alley with an extra horse for the prisoner. Tom Tyler's gang of miscreants had consisted of Tyler,

Barnes and four others. With Tyler already dead and the Barnes fellow incarcerated, that left four who might try to spring Barnes.

Four robbers against four lawmen. Even odds. As a matter of fact, he'd fought under worse...and more than once.

With the yawning emptiness in his gut as a reminder, he turned and moseyed back to the sheriff's office. A little supper wouldn't go amiss. He found Sheriff Tate and his two brothers engaged in a good-natured exchange, something to do with which one had the fastest horse.

The brotherly ribbing ceased when Sam entered. Tate nodded. "My brothers Nash and Luis," he said by way of introduction. With the same black hair and dark brown eyes, Nash could've been the sheriff's twin, except he lacked a couple of inches in height. Luis had inky black hair, worn longer and tied back with a rawhide braid. Taller than the sheriff, Luis was wiry where his two brothers were broad and muscular. His hooded eyes were a piercing gray. Sam doubted little passed unnoticed by the young deputy, if anything.

The two deputies acknowledged Sam with quick nods. "Marshal," Luis drawled. "Hope you're prepared for a fight. Word has it the rest of the gang is out for blood."

"Wouldn't expect any less," Sam said. "Where'd you get your information?"

Nash shot Sam a wolfish grin. "From none other than Barnes's baby sister."

"You sure about that?" Sam rubbed his chin, uneasy about Nash's source. "Doesn't make sense his own sister would turn on him."

"Reckon Miss Eleanor Barnes doesn't hold with his

bank-robbing, shooting-and-killing ways." Nash jutted his chin. "And I ought to know."

"Reckon you oughta at that." Luis jabbed his elbow in Nash's ribs. "Miss Ellie tell you where they might be hidin' out? 'Cause catchin' the bastards before they turn the town into a bloodbath trying to break Barnes out would be preferable...to my way of thinkin'."

Slowly, Sam nodded his approval. "Your brother's got a point. They have a hideout? Wouldn't be surprised if they used it again." He resisted the urge to tell 'em to shut the hell up. All this talk of hideouts and jailbreaks was keeping him from what had become his primary mission: finding Celine, or whatever she was calling herself now.

The sheriff raised an eyebrow. "A warren of old caves thought to be the site of played out silver mines. When Tom Tyler kidnapped his half-sister, they spent one night there before moving on." He stood and grabbed his Stetson from a hook, then set it on his head. "Wouldn't hurt to give it a look before the trial," Tate said, then turned to Sam. "Now. You ready for some supper?"

"A bite or two would go down fine." Hell, half a steer would be better, but whether he could manage eating after he confronted Celine was another thing entirely.

"Don't worry about our suppers," Nash called. "We're just the ones guarding your prisoner."

Tate chuckled. "Miz Foley will be taking care of your suppers. And you damn well know it."

Sam's foot tapped an erratic rhythm while the

sheriff gave last-minute instructions to his deputies. Soon he'd know if this woman was Celine or not. Had to be. Considering how fast she took off in that buggy, there was no room for doubt.

As the day passed and no irate US marshal banged at the door, Selma breathed a little easier. She and Star worked briskly on the baby garments, only interrupted each time Star took a quick breath or stiffened with a sudden twinge of pain.

"I'm fine...really," the redhead said, attempting to reassure Selma.

Selma pasted on a smile and nodded. "Good." But she wasn't reassured. She glanced down at her hands. Drat. They trembled ever so slightly as she placed a final hem stitch in the tiny gown.

"Sam should be home soon for his supper," Star said, trying to rise from the rocker.

The savory aroma of chicken stewing reached Selma's nose, causing her stomach to growl. She set the baby garment aside. "You stay put. I'll finish the meal. Just tell me what you want."

"There're just the dumplings to make. Are you sure you don't mind?"

"Of course not. I'll be only too happy to whip up some dumplings for our supper." Selma stood, then stretched the kinks from her back. "Dumplings it is, then."

She strode into the kitchen, grabbed a work smock off a hook, and quickly located the flour, lard and milk. She pulled a wooden bowl from the cupboard and worked the ingredients into a doughy consistency. After removing the chicken from the broth and setting it aside on a plate, she plopped spoonsful of the dough into the rich, bubbling broth. While the dumplings cooked, she separated the chicken from the bones and set the meat aside. Unable to resist sampling the tantalizing dish, she popped a morsel of tender chicken into her mouth. A small moan of satisfaction emerged before she could hold it back. "Delicious," she called to Star.

She wiped her floury hands on the smock. Once the dumplings had cooked and the broth thickened, she would add the chicken back into the broth and keep their dinner on a low fire until Star's husband came home.

Selma walked back into the front room and found Star peering through the window. "Cord's home," she said brightly. "And he has someone with him. I just hope there'll be enough chicken and dumplings to go around."

"Someone...with him?" Grabbing her throat, Selma barely choked the words out. It couldn't be... No, fate couldn't be so unkind. She sped to the window and watched with growing horror as the familiar tall, lanky figure of Sam Dunaway dismounted from his horse. Her knees grew so weak she grabbed the windowsill to steady herself. She took a quick, ragged breath, glancing over her shoulder. The back door beckoned. All she had to do was make a run for it. Should she? Gathering every ounce of courage, she stiffened her knees and spine. No. She'd run before, and look what that had done.

Face him now.

Courage gathered or not, she couldn't hold back

the nervous shudder racking her body. Every ambling step he took brought her world closer to disaster.

Beneath the shadow of his black Stetson, Sam's visage was schooled into a mask of determination. The clench of his jaw and the rigid set of his shoulders belied his long, easy stride. She knew that expression. He was steaming mad. Not that he didn't have a perfect right. He surely did.

The two men had stepped onto the porch and were shaking the trail dust from their clothing. All too soon, they were at the door before she could take another breath. Her mouth dried.

"Selma? What is it?"

"Wh-what?" Selma started at the touch of her friend's hand.

Pull yourself together.

"You're white as a sheet." Star slipped her hand over Selma's. "Your hands are freezing, and you're shaking like a leaf."

"I'm fine. Someone must've walked over my grave." And the man who might put her in that grave was, at this very moment, staring at her from the doorway. His upper lip twitched ever so slightly in a show of contempt. Or did she imagine it?

Star rushed to her husband's side and received a tender kiss on her forehead. Not wishing to intrude, Selma backed away. What she really wanted was to fade into the background—completely.

"My wife Star and her friend Miss Nelson," the sheriff said by way of an introduction. "This here's Marshal Dunaway. Here for the trial. Figured he could do with a home-cooked meal."

Directing his gaze toward Star, Sam removed his

Stetson. "Ma'am, I appreciate your hospitality. Don't go to any trouble on my account."

"No trouble at all, Marshal," Star said. "It's just chicken and dumplings."

"The dumplings!" Selma gasped, then darted from the room-anything to avoid the coming confrontation.

Once out of sight, she leaned against the wall to catch her breath. She fanned her burning cheeks while her heart raced like a runaway herd on the prairie. She peeked into the stewpot. The dumplings were perfectly puffy. Swiftly, she transferred the chicken back into the pot, then set it off the cooking plate.

What options did she have? None. Another deep breath. As calm as she could be under the circumstances, she grabbed another plate and silverware for the sheriff's guest. Gripping the implements tightly, she waltzed back into the sitting room and set them on the oak dining table.

Sam's gaze caught hers and held it. And like prey under the gaze of a cougar ready to pounce, she saw the anger seething beneath his seemingly polite expression, the tension at the corners of his eyes, and the telltale jittering muscle in his clenched jaw.

She swallowed the fear knotting her throat. "Marshal," she said, giving him a quick nod of acknowledgement.

"Thank you kindly, Miss-Nelson, was it?" One dark brow quirked, giving his expression an ironic twist.

A tiny nod was the most she could manage. Her heart thundered. She hid her trembling hands in the folds of her skirt. Not two feet away stood her worst nightmare. In the flesh. His anger so deep, so vibrant, she felt it roiling through him, sucking the air from the room.

Breathless, she gasped, "Air..." then rushed for the door and ran outside. Grabbing onto the first post, she clung to it, praying to awaken from the dream, all the time knowing it was no night terror but reality. A freshening wind blew through the cottonwoods and cooled her cheeks, but it did little to slow the rapid beating of her heart.

She started at the slamming of the screen door. Thinking Star had come to check on her, she turned to reassure her friend.

But no. Not Star.

Sam.

"Running out was rude, *Miss Nelson*." The heavy sarcasm in his tone sent a shiver up her spine.

She spun around, ready to bolt for her buggy, but Sam grabbed her wrist and pulled her close to his chest.

"I can explain," she gasped. After all this time, being near him still played havoc with her breathing. Her heart pounded like it would surely explode.

"Reckon you can." His voice was low and raspy in her ear, his breath warm and enticing on her neck. "And I'll bet it's a good 'un. But right now, you're gonna smile. Go back inside. Then sit down to supper and not burden your friends with our dirty little business. They'll know soon enough what you are, once I get around to arresting your sweet ass. Everyone will know you're a fraud and a thief."

"But—"

"Not another word. March," he ordered, pulling her along.

"Stop." She struggled to free her wrist from his iron grip. "Or they'll surely suspect something's wrong."

With a slow shake of his head, he released her. "You're a piece of work, Celine. You really are."

Stubbornly, she stopped and took a deep breath to calm herself. No one had called her by her real name in several years. Yet all too quickly, she experienced the familiar rush of heat to her core, as if they were readying for bed. The years since she'd last seen him dissolved into a blur of longing.

"Sam..." she managed to gasp, wanting—no, needing—to explain away her actions.

He grabbed her shoulders and shook her none too gently. "Save your breath. Nothing you say will make a damn bit of difference."

Stiffening her spine, she pushed away from him. Or tried to. "Get your hands off me. No matter what I've done, I'm still your wife. And as such, I deserve a bit of respect."

"Respect?" He sputtered with rage but freed her. "You lost all claims to mine when you ran off. A low-down thief in the night."

His handsome face darkened with anger, and his chest rose, tightening the shirt across his broad shoulders. "Like I said. Get inside and act like the lady you've somehow convinced these good folks you are."

Without another word, Selma raised her chin, straightened her skirts, and then swished inside. He'd never forget what she'd done.

Or forgive.

Back inside, and with more than a little trepidation, Selma faced her friends. The sheriff directed a frown at Sam, while a wide-eyed expression of concern occupied his wife's face. "Are you all right?"

Star moved slowly to Selma's side. "Why don't we sit ourselves down and have some supper."

Selma managed a tight smile just to reassure her friend. "I'm fine, darlin', and supper sounds like a fine idea." How she choked out the words without fainting, she didn't know. "Y'all sit. I'll bring in the chicken 'n' dumplings," she said, clutching her skirts to still her trembling hands.

It'd be a pure miracle if she didn't dump the entire meal into someone's lap.

Sam watched his wife—hell, that was who she was, no matter what she called herself now—scurry into the kitchen. Afraid she'd run right out the back door, he stood. "Maybe I oughta give her a hand."

"Oh no," the redhead said. "You're our guest. I'll check on her." She rose somewhat clumsily from the table, rubbing her lower back as she waddled into the kitchen.

From his spot, he could hear a flurry of whispers, but that was all. At least Celine hadn't run away...this time.

To his relief, the two women soon returned, both with flushed cheeks and tight smiles. Curious. Did the sheriff's wife already know about Celine's deceitful ways? Not likely. She seemed to be just what she was, a pretty—even when heavily pregnant—woman who adored her sheriff husband.

As for Celine, no matter how she tried to downplay her looks with a schoolmarm's bun and demeanor, there was no hiding her clear skin, so soft that even now he wanted to reach out and touch her. Eyes that sparkled with light like the summer sun on a mountain lake. Or the figure she'd tried to hide in a plain gray dress with its prim white cuffs and collar. Like a damn Pilgrim.

Celine set the heavy bowl of chicken and dumplings on the table. The sheriff's wife brought along a pan of golden-brown biscuits and set about arranging them in a fragrant stack. "I hope these turned out all right."

Sheriff Tate chuckled. "Don't pay my wife any mind, Marshal. She's fishing for a compliment. She knows makes the best biscuits in the county."

"Oh pooh. I'm sure the marshal doesn't care about that." Mrs. Tate sat, then turned to her husband. "Cord, would you say grace?"

The sheriff nodded. And during the short prayer, Sam experienced a pang of regret. Now this was a real family. By running off, Celine had stolen more than his life savings. She'd stolen his chance to have a home of his own with a passel of young 'uns. Stolen his very future.

"Amen."

Raising his head, he met Celine's gray gaze. She quickly glanced away, no doubt too ashamed to face him.

"Marshal, tell me, where do you hail from?" Mrs. Tate asked.

"Grew up in the Texas Panhandle," he said, reaching for a biscuit.

"Are you married? Have any children?" She rubbed her large belly. "This is our first."

"Now, Star, you're—"

"Oh hush, Cord. I get so few visitors out here. I like to know who I'm having dinner with."

Sam swallowed hard. "Ma'am, I *was* married, but

she was taken from me before we could have children."

Star gasped, ducking her head. "Oh, I'm so sorry."

Celine dropped her fork. "Sorry. How clumsy of me." Her cheeks reddening, she bent down to retrieve it, but Sam encircled her wrist with his hand. "Allow me." He picked it up.

She snatched the fork right from his hand. "I'll just find a clean one in the kitchen." She literally ran from the room. Sam tamped down a chuckle, amazed that touching her had flamed into the same white-hot spark of heat touching her always had.

In the kitchen, Selma stood in the back door and fanned her cheeks. Damn. Damn. Damn. How dare he touch her? Why had she run away in the first place? Maybe he would've understood the secrets she'd harbored for so long. No. She'd been afraid to take the risk that he'd turn on her and break her heart. Instead she'd chosen to break his. Selfish. Yes, indeed she'd been selfish. And cowardly. Anyway, it was too late now.

No wonder he couldn't forgive her. She couldn't forgive herself. But she could pay him back. Once her dressmaking business had begun to flourish, she'd set aside some money every month. She'd planned on sending it to him anonymously. He would've known it came from her, but it wouldn't have mattered.

"Need some help?" Star tapped Selma's shoulder and offered her a clean fork. She turned. "No, just catching a breath of air."

"What's wrong with you?" Star raised an eyebrow. "I've never seen you so discomfited. If I didn't know better, I'd think you knew the marshal. *Have* you met before?"

Was she that transparent? "Not now, Star. I'll tell you later when we're alone." She patted her friend's shoulder. "I'll be all right."

"He acts as if he knows you too," Star persisted. "And he's fairly bristling with anger."

"Please, just let it go...for now," she begged. "Please."

"I know he's a lawman and all, but he makes me very uneasy. I've never met anyone quite like him."

"Don't worry. He'd never hurt you, and the worst he can do is put me in jail." Her friend's eyes widened with surprise. "What?"

"Let's eat." Selma brushed by her friend, gripping the fork tightly.

Star followed and sat. "I'll have you gentlemen know you have Selma here to thank for this wonderful meal."

"Nonsense. All I did was make the dumplings. Star already had the chicken in the pot when I arrived. Delicious it is too. I just had to have a taste while I worked on the dumplings." Fancy just how ridiculous she sounded, prattling about tasting the chicken.

Sam nodded in Star's direction. "Appreciate the hospitality, ma'am."

"What do you think, Marshal, will there be a hanging or not?"

The sheriff frowned. "Star, that's not fit talk for the supper table."

Star continued, "Well, I hope he hangs. What you might not know, Marshal, is that Arvil Barnes is the one who shot my husband's first wife in a bank holdup."

"Star..." The sheriff's jaw clenched.

Sam nodded. "Yes, ma'am. I knew."

"Oh, then I guess I needn't say any more." Her cheeks turned a light pink.

The sheriff's weather-tanned face flushed as he uttered a terse "No. You don't."

"Miss Nelson, where're you from?" Sam shot her a mocking glance. "Did you grow up around here?"

She dared a quick glance in his direction, then focused on her plate. "No, I grew up in—" She tried to remember what she'd said before. His presence had her so upset she couldn't think. "Louisiana. I'm from Louisiana, Marshal."

"And how did you end up here in the Texas Hill country? A woman alone with her own business. Very *commendable.*"

That one was easy to answer since she'd told him the same story when they'd met. "I had a small bequest from one of my uncles who was a doctor. He also left me his horse and buggy. I've always had an aptitude with a needle, so I headed west. And here I am."

"And *here* you are." His tone dripped with sarcasm. Under the table, the muscles in her right thigh quivered. Damn him. He enjoyed tormenting her. Not that she didn't deserve it.

"Yes, Selma helped make my wedding dress," Star interjected, probably to diffuse the growing tension. "And now she's helping me with my baby's layette. I can do simple stuff, but Selma is a wonder."

"I'm beginning to see that," Sam said with a wry smile.

Clenching her jaw to keep from responding, Selma reached for a biscuit and buttered it. Cord passed the dumplings to Selma, who took only a small portion. Frankly, if she managed to swallow even a mouthful, her stomach was so uneasy, it might just return. Biting into the fluffy biscuit, she nearly choked. Her mouth was too dry to swallow. She reached for her glass of water and drank, relishing the sweet, cool water from the Tates' well.

"Are you all right, Selma?" her friend, her only real friend, asked.

"I'm fine. I was just-thirsty."

The rest of dinner passed as awkwardly as the first few minutes. Sam, sitting to her left, and a bewildered Star across. To Selma's right, the sheriff also appeared puzzled but thankfully kept his thoughts to himself.

As soon as she could do so politely, Selma rose and offered, "I'll clear the table and do the washing up. Goodness, Star," she said with a laugh. "With your belly, I'm amazed you can reach anything in the kitchen."

"Cord helps when he's here," Star said, directing a loving smile at her husband.

Sam stood, pushing his chair back. "Wouldn't mind having a look at your ranch, Tate, while the ladies are otherwise occupied." He nodded at Star.

Fine. Could he be any more obvious he didn't consider Selma a lady?

Cord rose. "Surely. We can smoke while we walk. The smoke bothers my wife."

As soon as the men left, Star pushed back from the table, stood and then wagged her finger in Selma's face. "You're not putting me off any longer. I want to know what's going on with you and that marshal."

Selma collapsed in the chair and hid her face in her hands. "I've told so many lies, I don't know what the truth is, or where it leaves off and the lies begin." Star placed her hands on Selma's shoulders. "I'm listening."

Tears streaming down her cheeks, she gazed up at her friend. "If I tell you the God's honest truth, I'll lose your friendship. And I can't bear that. Knowing you is the only thing that's made the last year livable."

"Now, I've told you all about how I pursued Cord. I was shameless."

"Oh honey, I've done so much worse."

Chapter Five

Sam took a long draw on his cigarette. "Nice spread you got here. Wouldn't mind settling down myself."

The sheriff stopped and faced Sam. "What's going on with you and our Miss Nelson?"

Sam exhaled. "Long story."

"I got time." Tate sat on an outcrop, leveling his no-nonsense gaze.

Sam took a long, thoughtful look around the rolling range. In the distance, the purple hills darkened against a glowing sky. He said nothing and took another drag.

"Miss Nelson's highly thought of round these parts," Tate said. "She's my wife's friend."

"So I gathered."

"And from the way y'all acted at dinner, you know each other. Got something against her? Know something we don't?"

"Could be."

"Where do you know her from?"

"A while back."

"Dammit, man! Is there a price on her head? Is

my wife in danger?"

"Your wife's in no danger from Celine."

"Celine?" Tate's forehead wrinkled.

"That was her name when I knew her."

"Hmph," Tate grunted. "Never thought Selma suited her." The sheriff took a long drag on his cheroot. "Lotta people come west. Reinvent themselves. How well did you know her?"

"Real well. Married her."

"Figured there had to be some kind of connection." He held up both hands in a gesture of surrender. "Forget I asked. Ain't about to poke my nose where it ain't needed."

"'Sall right. Came home from a trip. Found she'd cleared out. Took my savings."

"So our Miss Nelson's a common thief. Never would've figured. What're you gonna do about it?"

"When the trial's over, I'll arrest her." He kicked a rock with the toe of his boot just like he'd kick her out of his heart.

"She's set up a respectable life here."

"That's like her. She's sneaky and underhanded. A liar. Waited for the right moment and took off. Then a coupla months later, I heard she died in a boardinghouse fire in Amarillo. I went to see the body. Coulda been anybody's, but it was in the room she shared with another woman. Reckon it was Selma Nelson who died instead of Celine."

"Married long?"

"Year or so."

Tate stood. "I'd just as soon Star not know all this. I'll handle her after y'all are gone. But I don't want anything upsetting her. Not when she's so close to giving birth."

"Don't blame you." He threw down his smoke,

grinding it out with his boot heel. "What do you say we have a further look at your ranch? Then I'll pay my respects and go back to town."

"Might be best. Miss Nelson is supposed to stay with Star for a couple more days. Now that you've found her, do you think she'll run?"

"She's run before. Just need to get the trial over with. Judge Riordan won't arrive for at least a couple of days. Reckon the trial will take a day. I'll stick around until after the hanging, just in case any of his old gang have any thoughts of attempting a jailbreak."

Tate nodded. "Kinda like the idea of having another lawman around till then."

"Better odds."

While the water heated on the cookstove, Selma clasped her hands together to keep them from trembling. "So now you know everything. And I mean everything. You see why I had to leave, don't you?"

Star leaned against the wall and massaged her lower back with one hand. "Honey, I think you should've trusted your husband to stand beside you, no matter what."

"No man, especially a lawman, would understand who I was before." Selma opened a drawer and pulled out a dishrag. Anything to keep her hands busy.

"But don't you see you just made it worse by taking his money and running away? You were wrong about him. He still loves you."

"*Still*? All I saw in his eyes was hate and disgust. Telling him why I ran will only make it worse. Tonight,

I'll go back to the store, pack what I can in the buggy and leave town. I'll just have to start over somewhere else."

"In the night? No. You can't travel alone *at night*. No telling what might happen to you. No. No. No." She caught Selma's hands in her own, an expression of desperation on her face as she pleaded. "You promised to help me finish the baby clothes, and you have to keep that promise. Don't let me down, or I won't have a stitch to wrap my poor baby in."

Leave it to Star to add more guilt to Selma's already considerable pile.

"Then I'll sew like the wind. I *have* to get out of town before the trial's over. That's when he'll arrest me, take me back to Abilene and put me in jail."

"I don't think so. I can tell there's still something there in his heart. He's been hurt, but that doesn't mean he can't forgive you."

Selma set about stacking the dinner dishes, still wishing she'd run as soon as she'd first glimpsed her husband riding down Kenton Valley's main thoroughfare. "You don't know him like I do. He's a lawman, pure and simple. To his way of thinking, there's right and there's wrong. And there's *nothing* in between."

"Oh honey, surely not for someone he loved." Star gestured with a dismissive wave. "What you've told me isn't so bad. You couldn't help who your mother was or where you were born."

Selma unfolded and refolded the dishrag, finally setting it aside to face her friend. "I tried to put it behind me by leaving New Orleans after my mother died. I sold her house and headed west. Then I met Sam, and I thought that part of my life was over."

Star walked toward Selma. "Turn around," she ordered, then started to rub Selma's shoulders, easing the knots of tension. "Of course, leaving your husband was hurtful, and I'm not saying that taking his savings wasn't a bad thing to do. It was. But I believe if just tell him everything, he'll understand and forgive you. Besides, I bet he missed you more than the money."

"I don't know." Selma removed the pan of hot water from the cookstove and poured it into the large dishpan, then began to immerse the dirty dishes. "I've saved quite a bit from my dressmaking business. And I always meant to pay him back. But now I'm thinking I should keep it and go farther west-maybe up north. Yes—get out of Texas completely. I should've done that in the first place, but after the boardinghouse caught fire and everyone thought I was dead, I figured I was free to stay in Texas, and he'd have no reason to keep looking for me."

A wide smile creased Star's face. "Don't you see he was *meant* to find you? There's still hope. And you still have a chance to make it all up to him."

"Starlight Tate, anyone ever mention you have a weird way of looking at a situation? What I have a chance for is spending time behind bars. You don't reckon they'll hang me, do you?" she ended with a wail.

"Oh pooh. I don't reckon the marshal will even arrest you. Just give him a chance."

"I'm not the one who'll have to give him a chance. He has to give me a chance, and he's already made it clear no matter what I say, he's not having any of it."

"After Cord's wife and baby died, he was just as

certain he wouldn't risk marriage or having another child, but you see this"—she patted her belly— "don't you?" Star's blissful expression abruptly changed to a grimace as she clutched her lower belly. "That sort of hurt."

"Let's sit you down." Selma ran for a chair, then eased her friend down as gently as she could.

Giving a dismissive wave, Star said, "It's over. Just a twinge. Sign I'm getting closer." She favored Selma with a reassuring smile. "Anyway, that's what I've been told."

Anything but reassured, Selma argued, "You've been doing too much. Let's put you to bed."

"Oh no. If Cord came in and found me in bed, he'd go to pieces, certain that I'm at death's door." She paused with a dramatic hand to her forehead. "Losing his first wife and baby affected him a lot more than he ever lets on."

"When did you say that doctor's coming to town?"

"Any day now. I'll hold till then. First babies are always late." Star emitted a quiet grunt and bit her bottom lip.

"Another twinge?" Dear Heaven, what was she to do? Yes, she'd seen a baby or two born in the New Orleans brothel, but she'd never been part of the process. "Yeah, but it's nothing."

Nothing? Nothing was getting a hem length too long. *This* was so much more. Lives were at stake, and the doctor might be here *any day now*. "I think I'd better find your husband."

"There's no telling where they are. Cord's probably showing off his new bull. He's so proud of that creature you'd think he'd sired it himself."

Selma smiled at the comparison, but her friend's sense of humor didn't lessen the seriousness of her situation. "Why don't I just ring the dinner bell? That should get his attention."

Star gave her red curls a furious shake. "No, he'll think there's a real emergency."

Who knew her friend was so dad-blamed stubborn? "But it could be an emergency, and he'll come running. Isn't that what we want?"

Star held out her hand. "Just help me to the settee. If it'll make you happy, I'll put up my feet." Rising clumsily from her chair, she let out a soft grunt.

"Another?" *Oh damnation.* Sliding her arm around Star's waist, she eased her friend to the front room.

"You are such a dear and *such* a worrywart."

"And you're not worried enough."

"Life's too short to worry about everything. Besides, Cord does enough worrying for the both of us."

"At least someone in your family has some common sense."

Star grabbed the back of the settee and lowered her body into a sitting position. "How about a little help with my feet." She let out a chuckle. "It's been a while since I've seen them."

Distracted by the conflicting urges to run either for the hills or for a doctor, Selma sprang forward to pick up her friend's swollen feet. "Sorry."

"A pillow for my head and one for my feet. There might be an extra one in the chest at the foot of our bed."

"I'll be right back." Selma hiked up her skirts and ran for the stairs. She took one pillow from the bed and the other from the round-topped trunk. Unable to resist, she stopped long enough to admire the lacy curtains at the window. The high-backed oak bed and chest of drawers made for a cozy bedroom. Sheriff Tate had certainly provided a comfortable home for his wife.

Of course, Sam had planned on building them a new house, too-if she hadn't run off.

Be that as it may, Star deserved her happy home with her handsome husband.

Unlike Selma, who didn't deserve anything like a happy home. Or a husband. Or a family.

"Selma!"

Selma snapped out of her reverie. "Coming." She clasped the pillows to her chest and clambered downstairs. She discovered her friend with a panicked expression. "What's wrong?"

Chin trembling, Star said, "My water just broke."

Sam took in the distant cottonwood-covered hills and the lush grazing land. "The more I see of your ranch, the more impressed I am, Tate."

Tate nodded. "Used to be larger, but when my father died six months ago, my brothers and I split up the acreage. They've just started working their spreads. I had a head start because I was older and married. My foreman, Silas, looks after the place for me while I tend to business in town."

Nodding agreeably, Sam admitted, "I'd like a small spread someday. Wouldn't have to be as big as this." He emitted a rueful grunt. "I had plans, all right-lots of 'em. Reckon it's gonna take longer than I figured. Thanks to Celine."

Tate removed his Stetson, untied his bandanna, then mopped his forehead with it. "What're ya going to do about Miss Nelson—Celine, I mean? You really mean to put her in jail? Have a trial? Wash your long johns in public?"

"Hell, I don't know. If she were a man, I'd have no problem making her pay. Horsewhipping's too good for a no-account thief."

"Might've had a good reason. Maybe ought to ask her."

"I'm sure she'll have a mighty fine tale to tell."

"What would it hurt to listen? Doesn't mean you have to believe her."

"Reckon—" He broke off at the sound of the dinner bell being rung with fervor.

The sheriff set his hat on his head, dug in his heels, and broke into a dead run. "Gotta be something wrong with my wife," he said over his shoulder.

Sam took off after the lawman. The bell being rung this long after dinner was a sure sign of some kind of trouble. Fire or, in earlier times, a native uprising. Most likely the sheriff was right about there being trouble with his pregnant wife. Easy to see how much the young couple loved each other. Hell, once upon a time, he'd loved Celine just as much. Wanted to give her the world too.

As they rounded the barn, Sam spied Celine banging the bell with every ounce of strength she had.

"It's Star," she yelled. "The baby's coming."

The two men ran inside. Tate's tanned cheeks were pale, and he looked as if he might collapse. He rushed to his wife's side, kneeling and clasping her hand.

Sam glanced around, wondering if there was something he oughta be doing.

Celine tugged on the sheriff's elbow. "We've got to get her upstairs. She needs to be in bed."

"It's too soon," Star wailed. "Can't we stop it?"

"No, honey," Celine said, stroking Star's hair back from her face. "Once it's started, there's nothing anyone can do."

Tate nodded, then, sweeping his wife into his arms, he carried her upstairs.

Hell, Sam wondered, what was he supposed to do now? Surely he didn't have any business hanging around. He set his hat on the table.

Celine shot him a bewildered expression before rushing after the sheriff and his wife. Damn. Was he supposed to be some kind of mind reader? What should he be doing?

Boil water? Wasn't that what they always did? Who the hell knew what the water was for? He sure didn't.

He ought to go for help, but being a stranger in Kenton Valley, the best he could do was go back to town and get the sheriff's brothers, who would likely be more useless than he was. Besides, they had the prisoner to guard.

He ambled into the kitchen and grabbed the large kettle from the stove.

Outside at the well, he dropped the wooden bucket, hearing a gratifying splash as the bucket landed. He turned the hand crank, pulled the bucket up, and then poured the contents into the kettle. Damn. No one ever said how much water to boil. Lord, but he was as useless as teats on a boar.

Birthing babies was women's work. As far as he knew,

Celine had precious little experience in that line. While he was trying to figure out his next move, he heard a flurry of footsteps down the stairs. Celine's, from the sound of them.

"What are you doing just standing there? Get that fire heated up and get that water boiling!" She shot him an exasperated look. "And one kettle's not enough."

Whoa. Who was this fierce woman ordering him around in a kitchen not her own? Sticking his hands in his pockets, he said, "This is my first birthing."

"You were always good at stating the obvious. Anyway, it's not mine, so move your stumps."

Not her first birth? What in Hades did she mean by that? Had she been around when another woman gave birth, or had she actually given birth? Questions for another time.

"We need Mrs. Crayton from the next spread over. This baby's coming."

Next spread over? In Texas terms, that might mean twenty or a hundred miles. "I-uh, which way? Give me a general direction."

"Damnation." She groaned her dissatisfaction. "You'll never find the place. The sheriff will have to go...if I can get him to leave. Just boil the damn water." Without another word, she spun and rushed back upstairs.

Who was this so-called seamstress? The longer he was around her, the more of a stranger she became. For one, during the year they were married, he'd never heard her so much as utter a curse word-much less order him around as if he were her servant.

He set the kettle on the cookstove, then opened the door. Inside the stove, the embers still glowed from supper. He pulled three lengths of chopped wood from the bucket beside the stove and added them. Thankfully, the firewood caught quickly. *"More water,"* that was what she'd said. He looked around for a larger container to boil water in.

Stepping outside onto the back stoop, he spied a washtub hanging from a nail. *That oughta do it.*

After filling the washtub from the well and setting it on the stove, he rubbed his hands on his denim trousers. At least that much was done.

Maybe he ought to see what was going on upstairs. See if Celine had any more orders. Damn if this wasn't the craziest situation he'd ever come across.

With some reluctance, he climbed the stairs, then tapped on the bedroom door.

Celine whipped the door open and stepped into the narrow hall. "What do you want now?"

"Just checking to see if there's anything I else I can do."

"You can talk the sheriff into going for help. He doesn't want to leave her."

"Can't imagine why. I'd be damn nervous if my baby was about to be delivered by a lying, thieving seamstress."

"You didn't tell him. Please say you didn't."

He remained silent as her gray eyes searched his face for the answer. "You did! Damn you!"

"He would've known anyway as soon as I arrested your ass."

"No. You didn't have to tell him *now*. You could've waited." She waved her hands in the air. "I don't have time for this. *You* see to the water. You're not needed up here."

She spun around, entered the bedroom and firmly shut the door in his face.

Nothing else to do, he headed downstairs. The water was starting to simmer. *Good. That ought to make her happy.*

The sound of a heavier tread on the stairs alerted Sam to Tate's arrival. "I've got to get help. Crayton's Double Bar X Ranch is fifteen miles as the crow flies."

Sam squinted at the darkening sky outside the window. "Not much of a moon."

"Right. Can't risk my horse. I'll have to go the longer way around." Tate sat heavily, studying the floor between his boots. "Damn it. I thought I had everything under control. The new doc is scheduled to arrive in town tomorrow or the day after. Once he arrived, I wouldn't have had to worry about *this* baby. This time would be different."

"Would a doctor have made a difference? Understand she was gut shot."

"True. And the baby was just a little thing, too early to live. I've been worried sick about Star, but when the new doctor agreed to settle here with his family, I thought I could quit worrying."

Sam clapped Tate on the shoulder. "Appears to me that your wife is further along than your first. Appears strong and healthy."

"Yes, but it's still early."

"I'll stay here and help Celine." Sam emitted a bark of laughter. "At least I'll be here to follow her orders."

Chuckling, Tate stood, picking up his Stetson. "You sure you want to arrest her? She's a hell of a woman."

Sam sniffed. "You'd do better to tend your business and let me tend to mine."

"'Nuff said." Tate jammed his Stetson onto his head and took off into the night.

Sam watched until the sheriff disappeared from sight. Hell of a woman? Hmph. Hell of a thief.

Selma wiped the perspiration from Star's forehead with a damp cloth. "Don't fight the pain. Try to take some deep breaths."

"What do you know about it?" Star scowled while she pushed up on her elbows, shifting her position again. "This hurts a lot. A lot more than I thought it would."

"Yeah." Selma plumped her friend's pillow. "You have a long night ahead, and you're going to hurt a lot more before you're through."

Star frowned. "Don't remind me. Gosh, I hope Cord will be all right. I worry about him riding out in the dark."

"He'll be fine. I would've sent Sam, but he would've surely gotten lost." Selma straightened her friend's bed linens. "Besides, we don't need either one of those men here underfoot."

"Are you sure you know what you're doing?"

"I saw several babies delivered at my mother's house," she said, exaggerating a bit.

Star's brows drew together in a frown. "I guess it must happen occasionally. Wonder why it doesn't happen more often. "

"There're herbs and such." Selma sat on a chair beside the bed, but kept holding her friend's hand. "But sometimes it's too late for them to do any good."

"Yeow!" Tensing up, Star grabbed her belly.

"Come on now, breathe through it. They're coming pretty regular. I think this little one is eager to come into the world and see his pretty mama and handsome papa."

Star ran her hand through her mop of sweat-dampened curls. "The way I look now, I'll probably scare the little tyke to death." She relaxed her grip on Selma's hand as the pain seemed to fade. "It's just as well Cord's not here. He's petrified something will go wrong."

"Men clearly have no understanding of such things. You're young and healthy, and your baby will be a little early, but we'll keep him nice and warm."

"He? You think it's a boy."

"You're carrying high and round like you stuffed a pumpkin up the front of your dress. Just an old wives' tale, but sometimes they hold a kernel of truth."

"At your mother's *house*, did you actually help *deliver* the babies?"

"Well-uh, no. I watched, through the French doors from the balcony, concealed behind a curtain. But I assure you the details are extremely vivid in my mind." She patted Star's hand, hoping it would reassure them both.

Star's gaze widened. "But what if something goes wrong? Would you know what to do?" Selma hesitated, hating to admit the truth. "No, but that's why I sent your husband after

Mrs. Crayton. She's brought dozens into this world, or so I've heard told."

"It's true. She delivered me."

Selma fluffed the pillow just as Star winced. "No, not another one."

And so the night passed ever so slowly with Star's contractions increasing in intensity and duration. Stretching to relax the muscles in her back, Selma took a moment to glance at the small timepiece she always kept pinned to her shirtwaist bodice.

"What time is it?" Star asked, the anxiety plainly written across her face.

"Nearly midnight."

"Why hasn't Cord come back with Mrs. Crayton?"

"I'm sure he'll return any minute."

"But I want him *now*. I need him. Dammit! I can't stand this pain much longer. Just do something. Get this baby *out* of me." Star twisted her hands in the sheets. "I'm thirsty. I'm going to die if this baby doesn't come out soon. Please. Take it out!"

One thing Selma had observed witnessing the births at her mother's house was that the two women both became desperate, irritable and almost irrational right before the really hard work of birthing a baby began. Matters had progressed rapidly if her friend was already at that stage.

"I've got to get up." Star twisted around in the bed, pulling back the linens.

"No, not yet."

"What do you know? You know *nothing* about how bad I hurt. I need the chamber pot!"

"That means the baby is moving into the birth canal." At least that was what she hoped it meant. "It's time to push."

Where was the sheriff anyway? And where was the midwife? She opened the bedroom door and yelled, "Sam! I need some help up here."

Chapter Six

Sam ran for the stairs. "I'm coming. Are you ready for the instruments?"

He'd already boiled the scissors and twine, apparently for cutting and tying off the cord. Celine had already had him gather all the clean linens and stack them in the room, including soft flannel blankets and nappies. Everything was ready for the infant about to be born in the room over his head. How did women stand it? Screeching cries gave way to whimpers, only to start all over again when the birth pangs renewed.

Somewhat grudgingly, he had to admire the way Celine kept a cool head through everything.

How much longer? Would the midwife get here in time to deliver the baby, or would it all be left up to an inexperienced seamstress? He tapped on the door.

Celine stuck her head out. "Yes, I need the scissors and twine. It won't be much longer."

"How long is that?"

"Maybe an hour or less, since the baby is on the small side."

He wrapped up the scissors and twine in a clean pillowcase and carried them back upstairs.

"I'm going to need you to stay with me."

"What?"

"She's ready to push. You stand at her head and, mind you, keep your eyes on her face. I'll take care of business on this end."

"Yes, you will. You certainly will." Using his forearm, he wiped the sweat from his brow. Damn, never figured on being this close to such goings-on.

He stood by the young woman's head and took her hand in his. She grabbed on to his hand, gripping like a steel vise, and began to grunt.

Oh Lord, what was he doing here? Fathers were supposed to be somewhere else, pacing the floor or drunk out of their minds. But he wasn't the father and hadn't dared get drunk in case Celine needed him for something. "*Keep a clear head*" was what she'd said.

"Whenever you feel the pressure, take a deep breath, hold it, and then push with all your might."

Star whipped her head from side to side. "I can't. It hurts too much."

"You have to. That's the only way this baby is coming out, Star. You *have* to push."

Cord reached the Crayton ranch in record time, considering there was no moon and taking great care not to injure his buckskin gelding.

He patted the horse's neck. "Good job, Winchester." As late as it was, he could see the flickering light of a kerosene lamp inside the Crayton ranch house.

He dismounted, tied up the gelding, then stepped

onto the porch. The door opened before he could knock. A grizzled older man stood there holding a shotgun. "Who goes there?"

Cord stepped back. "Sheriff Tate," he said, identifying himself. "I need your missus. My wife's time has come."

"The missus ain't back from Mrs. Holt's lying-in. Wife's been gone all day. That's why I'm still up. Don't cotton to her coming back to a dark house."

Fear sliced through Cord's gut. Fear that shook him down to his boots and threatened to turn his guts to water. "I got to get back, then."

"You left her alone?"

"No. Miss Nelson's with her."

"Don't reckon any spinster lady knows anything about—" The rancher cut off, shaking his wiry head.

Cord reined in his impatience. "I got to get back to them. Sorry for disturbing you."

He ran from the porch to his horse, untied the gelding, placed his boot in the stirrup and mounted.

"I'll bring her over as soon as she gets home," the rancher called after Cord.

"Appreciate it," Cord called over his shoulder.

Damnation. All his plans were for naught. The doctor hadn't arrived, and Mrs. Crayton wasn't available either. That good woman had delivered more than half the babies in the county, including his first wife's, who died under Mrs. Crayton's care through no fault of her own.

He spurred the gelding forward. He had to get home before it was too late. He couldn't lose Star. Not another wife and baby. God couldn't be so cruel. Could he?

*

Selma lifted the sheet, keeping one eye on Sam. "I can see the head."

"Really?" Eyes wide, he cut his gaze to hers.

"Shut up, Sam. Support her back and look anywhere but here." She fixed him with a stony expression. "Now, Star, with this next pang, grasp your knees and push."

"No! I can't push." Star whipped her head back and forth. "It hurts too much." She let out a low, guttural groan.

As the baby's head began to crown, Selma supported the tissues most likely to tear with a firm hand. "Stop pushing. Pant like a dog."

Star complied, then Selma gently eased the delicate skin around the baby's head. Miracle of miracles, the tender tissues remained intact. "All right now, almost done." She maneuvered one tiny shoulder and then the other. The rest of the baby slipped out with ease. Star collapsed back on the pillow, heaving a sigh of relief.

Selma held the baby up by his heels. "It's a boy! A redheaded baby boy."

The baby let out a squall that surely could've been heard for miles.

"Is he all right?" Star asked.

"He's perfect." Selma turned to Sam. "You can leave. You're no longer needed."

"Gladly." He jumped to his feet and made tracks for the door.

Selma quickly cleaned the secretions from the babe's face, cut and tied off the cord, then wrapped him in a blanket and placed him in Star's waiting arms. "Put him to your breast. You won't have milk yet, but my mother's midwife said doing so would help the afterbirth pass."

The baby latched on, and Starr let out a yelp. "I'll say. I feel like I'm having another baby."

"Good." The afterbirth slipped out easily, then Selma reached under the sheet and massaged Star's belly until Selma felt the womb had tightened. As far as she knew, the womb would need periodic massaging for the next twenty-four hours or so.

"Thank you, Selma. I don't know what I would've done without you. My husband would've been useless."

Selma wiped the perspiration from her brow. "I'm glad I was here and had half a notion of what to do."

"He's so beautiful."

"Who, Cord?"

"No, silly. My baby boy," Star said with a contented smile. "I do wish he hadn't been born with red hair, though. That means he'll have my bad temper."

"Hmph. When it comes down to it, most men have bad tempers when the occasion calls for it. Now, let's get you and the baby cleaned up. Won't the sheriff be surprised when he comes home to find you and your baby safe and sound?"

"I imagine he'll be greatly relieved."

"Hand him over so I can finishing cleaning him up." When she'd finished cleaning the squirming baby boy, she said, "You know, he's not quite as small as I expected he'd be."

"We might've had a tiny head start before we tied the knot," Star said, her eyes sparkling with humor.

"Now, that's nobody's business but your own." She

handed the baby back to Star, who commenced examining his fingers and toes. "He's perfect."

"Yes, he is. Thank the Lord for that."

A light knock sounded. Selma whipped the door open. "What do you want?"

Sam held his hands up in surrender. "Just checking to see everything's all right."

"Everything's fine in here. Now go on. While you're at it, a cup of coffee wouldn't go amiss."

"Yes, ma'am." He saluted and clicked his heels. "You're mighty bossy."

"I've just brought the sheriff's son into the world. I think I have a right to be a little bossy. Now go on." She shut the door and turned to face her friend.

"You're so mean to him. And I know you don't mean to be, because it's obvious to me you still love him."

"You'd be mean too, if he was going to arrest you when this is all over with."

"You don't believe he'd do something like that, do you?"

"I most certainly do. In Sam's mind, there's right, and there's wrong. And this lawman doesn't care about in-between."

"Then we'll have to get you out of town. You could go back to New Orleans. You could start over."

"Not New Orleans. I know too many people there."

"What about New York?"

Selma sank wearily into the rocking chair. "Honestly, I think he'd chase me to the ends of the earth. Running would mean taking all I've saved to pay him back and starting over again. I got so tired of running. Besides, I really like Kenton Valley."

"It's true that you've become a valued member of our community. You're respected. And you're my best friend." Star glanced down lovingly at the baby in her arms. "You brought my baby into this world."

Selma flashed a smile. "More than anything, I will always value your friendship. But think how the town would turn against me if it were to become known my mother was an infamous New Orleans madam, and I grew up in her brothel."

"No one's going to find that out from me." Star kissed the baby's fingers one by one before continuing. "Still, you should've trusted Sam with your secret."

Unable to relax, Selma leaned forward, her elbows on her knees, her hands clasped. "It wasn't just Sam that Thibodaux would've told. He would've spread it all over Abilene unless I slept with him. He was one of the reasons I left New Orleans, but he was so obsessed he even followed me to Abilene. I might have grown up in the brothel, but I didn't work in it. Besides, that distinction wouldn't have mattered. Why would anyone believe me if the former lieutenant governor of Louisiana declared otherwise?"

"I see your point."

"Sam was away, and I didn't know when he'd be home again. I couldn't wait. I had to leave."

"Well, you're in a pickle for sure."

"Feels like I was born in a pickle," Selma said with a rueful chuckle. "Now, let's discuss something more pleasant. What are you going to name your son?"

*

Downstairs, Sam took the coffeepot off the cook plate, then opened a cupboard to find a clean cup, muttering as he did.

"A cup of coffee wouldn't go amiss."

Since when had he become Celine's servant? Blazes.

Who the hell did she think she was, anyway? He didn't even know who she was anymore.

All the passion he'd felt when they were together was still there, if his stiff prick was any indication. And some of the tenderness remained. It was easy to see from Celine's pale cheeks and drooping shoulders just how exhausted she was. Somehow, a slender seamstress who'd never had a child had brought the sheriff's wife safely through her labor with a healthy baby boy as the result. Now, the sheriff had a fine, strapping son. Probably the first of many.

What Sam wouldn't have given to have at least one of his own. His father had been killed in the Civil War when Sam was just a baby, but his ma had married again, this time to a Texas Ranger, when Sam was ten. His stepfather had been a good man, but there'd been no more children. What would it have been like to have a whole passel of brothers and sisters? He'd always dreamed of having a family with lots of kids, and when he'd married Celine, he'd been certain his dream would come true.

Damn her!

Chapter Seven

The sky had begun to lighten when Sam heard the hoofbeats of an approaching rider. He picked up the shotgun, stood beside the front door and opened it. Recognizing the sheriff's buckskin gelding, Sam set the weapon down in its usual place. The sheriff had galloped back like a man possessed.

"Is my wife all right?" Tate asked, stumbling onto the porch. "The midwife was away with another lying-in. How's Star?"

Sam stepped back, allowing the sheriff to enter. "Your wife's fine...if a little wore out. But she ought to be the one to tell you the news."

"Hot damn!" Grinning, the sheriff ran for the stairs, and Sam followed.

Celine met the men in the hall, leaving the door open for the sheriff. "Let's give them their privacy," she said to Sam, shutting the door behind her.

Outside the room, Sam heard the sheriff let out a whoop of excitement. A thread of envy wormed its way in his gut. He turned to Celine. "You did a good deed this night. Too bad you couldn't find it in your heart to stick around for our family. We could've had ours started by now."

"This isn't the time, Sam," she said, heading downstairs.

"Why not?" He followed her. Time they got it all out in the open. "Were you always a lying, thieving bitch, or did you just hate me that much?"

"Oh, Sam, it wasn't about you at all." She sighed. Her shoulders drooped with fatigue. "I need to rest for a few minutes. It's too long a story to go into now."

"Hmph. You'll have plenty of time to tell it to a judge. He'll listen."

She stopped at the bottom step and turned to face him. "Are you really going to arrest me? Would you go that far?" She gazed up at him, her clear gray eyes seemingly full of love.

His heart clenched in his chest, weakening his knees. No. He squared his shoulders. No way would he let her sucker him into falling for her again. "Damn straight, I'll arrest you."

She sighed again, walked over to the settee and sat. "I really could use that cup of coffee." Sam held back a growl. If coffee was what she wanted, then coffee she'd get. He strode to the kitchen and poured a cup. When he returned, he found her sound asleep.

Fine. Sleep all you want, but there'll come a time for reckoning. Indeed there will.

Raising the cup to his lips, he swilled the brew down himself. Ugh. Time to make a fresh pot. The sheriff would need a cup when he came down from getting acquainted with his new son.

He watched her sleep the sleep of innocence. How

infuriating, when he knew full well she was anything but. When the sheriff came downstairs, Celine awoke. She sat up and glanced around, rubbing the sleep from her eyes.

Sam nodded. "Glad you could join us now that you've had your beauty sleep."

The smile on Tate's face spread from ear to ear. "Think we need to celebrate," he said, opening a chest and pulling out a bottle of whiskey and two cigars. "I saved these special for this day." He poured two shots, then handed one to Sam, along with a cigar.

Sam downed a shot of the whiskey. "Good stuff, Sheriff."

"The best Tennessee has to offer." Tate lit his cigar, taking a draw.

"Sorry. I didn't mean to fall asleep." Celine stood, straightening her skirts. "I'd best see how Star and the baby are."

"You haven't been asleep that long," the sheriff said. "I just left them a few minutes ago." "Still...I'd best see to them."

Sam took a puff on his cigar, casting his gaze at Celine's slender waist.

When Celine was out of earshot, the sheriff poured another shot. "You're not going to arrest her, are you?"

"Yep.".

"Has she explained? Star told me Miss Nelson was aiming to pay you back and that she had a good reason. Of course, she declined to share that reason with me."

"Well, Celine hasn't bothered to share it with me either, and until she does, she's still a lying, no-account thief."

"That's harsh. Would that kind of woman have

bothered to help my wife?"

Sam shrugged. "Who knows?" Indeed, he was beginning to doubt whether or not he'd be able to arrest her. Seeing her again had left him in a state of confusion. Why couldn't she just have stayed dead? Life was much simpler that way. A lawman had to stand for something, and if it wasn't for law and order, then what was the point of wearing a badge?

Selma stood at the back door, watching the sun rise on a day full of promise. The great state of Texas had a new citizen, and the Tate family would flourish and grow. There would be many more children—Selma was certain, given the love that fairly blinded one when the sheriff and his wife gazed into each other's eyes.

She'd once looked into Sam's eyes that way, and he hers. Sighing, she folded the dishtowel. She'd made so many mistakes, and now it was too late. Even if she could make Sam understand why she'd acted so, he'd still arrest her. That was the kind of lawman he was.

Unable to find any additional reasons to avoid facing him, she walked into the front room. "Gentlemen." Sam gave her a deadpan expression, but the new father beamed. Without another word, she took their dirty plates and cups with her to the kitchen and set them into the dishpan. After adding more wood to the fire, she hefted the kettle onto the cookstove, then returned to the dishpan for a cup.

"Celine."

Selma started at the sound of his voice so close

behind her and dropped the cup at his feet. As she knelt down to retrieve it, he caught her wrist, bringing her back to her feet.

"Sorry. I didn't mean to startle you."

"Then why are you coming up behind me, cornering me here in the kitchen? I thought you and the sheriff were going back to town this morning."

"We are, but I wanted to say—"

"Say what? There's nothing to say. I stole your money and ran off. I had a reason, which doesn't seem so important now, but that doesn't alter the facts of what I did. I've accepted that you're going to arrest me after the trial."

"We don't have to hash this over now. You were up most of the night. You're all tuckered out. We can talk later about what happens next." His tone was almost tender.

She ducked her head. "I know it doesn't make any difference, but I *am* sorry."

"No. It doesn't make any difference—not in the eyes of the law."

"And the law is all that matters...to you."

He gripped her wrist. Was that a tremor she felt? "What about in your eyes, Sam? You're more than a lawman. You're a man. And *I'm your wife.*"

His gaze narrowed. He clenched his jaw, then released her wrist as if he'd burned himself.

"I didn't think so," she said bitterly, turning from him. "You're a lawman, through and through."

Before Sam could respond, the sheriff called out, "Ready to ride?"

"Coming." Sam cut his gaze back to hers. "Later."

"By all means, *later.*" She watched him turn and leave

the kitchen, his shoulders squared as if she meant nothing. Tears stung her eyes. For a moment, she thought he'd softened toward her, but nothing had changed in his hard-as-nails attitude.

Nothing.

She bit her lips to keep from crying. Crying wouldn't solve anything. Never had. Never would.

Selma hung the dishtowel over the edge of a drawer and closed it. On reflection, the morning had sped by. Breakfast for four, then the men left to go to town. Baths for Star and the new baby, then the dishes. Now, there were eggs to gather and chickens to feed. She picked up the egg basket and stepped outside onto the back stoop, breathing in the fresh morning air.

Then she caught the odor of something not quite so fresh.

"Don't move, missy." An arm grabbed her roughly. The cold metal of a gun barrel shoved at the notch behind her ear.

"I won't. What do you want? We don't have much money in the house, but you can have what there is."

The stranger chuckled, and an eerie sensation prickled her skin. "Didn't expect the sheriff's wife to be so obliging."

"I'm not the sheriff's wife. I'm here to help her with…"

"With what?"

"She's just had a baby last night." Her breath caught in her throat. She'd said too much. "So there's three of ya here? Is that all?"

Damn her loose tongue. She'd just told this outlaw how vulnerable they were. Reluctantly, Selma nodded. "Yes."

"Back in the house." He shoved her inside, then forced her from the kitchen into the front room.

She turned to get a look at him. Long, oily blond hair and beady brown eyes. And one very nasty mustache. "Who are you?"

"Name's Booker Hunt." Two more men entered through the front door. How had these men dared to break into the sheriff's home? They must've been watching for the men to leave.

"This here's Dooley Fisher." Fisher stepped forward, sweeping his cowboy hat off. Lank brown hair fell in his face. He snorted and swept it back, then covered his head again. "The other is Mad Dog O'Reilly. He's a little crazy, so don't mess with him none."

Mad Dog's hair was ginger red, his eyes a washed-out, pale blue that glinted with madness. "Name's Kevin, ma'am," he said with a light Irish brogue. "Don't be payin' that Mad Dog business any mind."

"If you don't want money, what do you want?" she asked, trying to keep the fear from her voice. "Food? Are you hungry? The stove's still hot. I can fix more breakfast."

"Well, isn't she the gracious hostess?" O'Reilly said. "Oh, I be hungry all right, but it's not your cookin' I fancy." He stepped forward, his gaze focused on her breasts. Now there was more expression in his demented blue eyes, and it wasn't one that offered any reassurance.

The squall of a baby rent the air, stopping O'Reilly in his tracks.

Selma swallowed hard. "I have to check on the baby. May I?" She looked to Hunt for his approval, since he seemed to be the leader of the bunch.

He nodded.

"Smart, she is. I like me women smart," she heard O'Reilly say as she fled upstairs. *Think. Think.* Her six-shooter was secreted in her sewing basket. Could she get to it in time? Could she use it if she did?

"Go with her, Mad Dog. Make sure they don't have any weapons up there. Dooley, you know what you have to do. Go on."

O'Reilly was behind her, breathing down her neck before she could even get the door open. At the door, she turned to face him. "Leave this to me, Mr. O'Reilly. I don't want you to scare Mrs. Tate half to death. Let me explain your presence before she sees you."

He cocked his head to the side. "Do you think I'm so frightful, then?"

"No woman is going to be pleased to have gun-toting strangers in her home, especially a woman who's just had a baby. *Please*...wait here."

Selma opened the door and slipped inside the room. "Are you all right?"

"Other than I feel like I've ridden bareback from Llano to Kenton Valley, I'm fine."

"Really?" Selma permitted herself a smile. "I guess childbirth must feel like it at that."

She moved closer to the bed and said in a low undertone, "Does your husband keep any weapons in this room?"

Star's eyes widened. "What a strange question. Yes, there's a second shotgun under the bed. Why?"

"We need to hide it under the feather tick. There are three men who've taken us hostage. I have a feeling they're part of your brother's old gang. One of them is outside waiting to search the room. Anything else?" Selma crouched down and pulled the shotgun from underneath the bed, then hurriedly lifted the side of the feather tick and shoved it under, then smoothed the bed linens over it.

"Not that I know of. Have they hurt you?" Star struggled to sit.

"No. You *must* stay in bed. Pretend to be weak as a kitten. What we don't want is for them to take us with them."

Star nodded. "My brother Tommy, God rot his soul, kidnapped me once and carted me off like a sack of feed. No, we don't want a repeat of *that*."

O'Reilly banged on the door. "Enough!"

The baby let out a squall. Selma picked up the baby and handed him to Star, then rushed to the door. Selma opened it. "See what you've done, Mr. O'Reilly? You've awakened the baby. Please remember that this is neither a saloon nor a brothel. It's a woman's home."

"And 'tis you who'd be remindin' me, is it?"

"Yes, indeed I am, sir." Even if he were the furthest thing from a gentleman, perhaps treating him like one would influence him to act like one. It was a slim hope at best, but it was all she had.

"You may enter. Mrs. Tate, this is Mr. O'Reilly. He's one of the gentlemen who wishes to force your husband to release the man who killed a defenseless woman."

Playing her role to the hilt, Star laid her head on the pillow as she weakly said, "I don't remember you from my brother's gang."

"No, ma'am. I wasn't in these parts when that event occurred. I met Booker and Dooley afterwards. Now enough of this polite shite. Do ye be keepin' any guns or knives in here?"

"In *my* bedroom? I assure you I do not."

"Then ye won't be mindin' if I have a look around."

"Go ahead." Star gestured with a limp wave. Good, she was playing her part of invalid well.

He strode over to the wardrobe and opened it, rooted around, then closed the door. He got down on his knees and peered under the bed.

Star's hands move restlessly over the bed linens.

Careful. Don't give it away.

O'Reilly reached for the counterpane and whipped it back.

"Please, Mr. O'Reilly!" Star protested her outrage, clutching what remained of the bed linens to her chest.

A cagey expression crossed his face.

Selma held her breath when he reached down and ran his hands along the feather tick. "Now, now. What have we here? I wouldn't have thought such two fine ladies as yerselves would lie to a gentleman." He yanked out the shotgun by its barrel.

Selma's heart sank to her knees. "You can't blame us for trying," she said with a nervous fluttering of her hands.

"Oh, I'll not be blamin' the sheriff's wife. This wasn't her doin'." Still holding the shotgun by the barrel, he strode close to Selma, forcing her back against the wall. "Yer the one I'll be blaming, and ye'll be paying for yer audacity, never fear."

She averted her face from his. His breath was rank with the smell of stale coffee and cigarettes. She squared her shoulders. "Take a step back, Mr. O'Reilly. I find your manners offensive and your breath more so."

"Oh ye do, do ye?'" He took another step closer, his gaze full of madness.

Chapter Eight

It was almost noon, and Eleanor Barnes knelt in her garden, pulling weeds with a vengeance. She stood for a moment, rubbing the aching muscles in her lower back. Pulling weeds was a mundane chore, but as such, it kept her from thinking about her no-good brother waiting for trial. There'd been at least five good citizens of Kenton Valley in the bank the morning the Tyler gang decided to rob it. And all five had seen her brother, Arvil, shoot Annie Tate in her pregnant belly. The coming trial was just a formality. He would hang for certain.

The sooner it was over with, the better.

Then she wouldn't be tempted to think back about her big brother before he became a bank robber. How he'd taught her to sit a horse, or where to find the best swimming hole or the sweetest peaches in all of Texas. No, she didn't want to think about that brother at all.

She knelt again and began ripping the weeds from the green-onion patch. So intent on her task was she that she didn't hear the intruder until she was rudely picked up and swung around to face one of her brother's old gang.

"Dooley Fisher," she hissed. "You'd better get out of here. The sheriff and a US marshal are all looking for you and the rest of you low-down miscreants."

"That's a mighty smart mouth you have, Ellie. You need to take a message to the sheriff and be damned quick about it."

"Oh? Are you turning yourself in?" she asked, not quite believing he'd be so foolish. "Hell, no." He released her. "We want Arvil released, and this message will do the trick."

"You're crazy—not to mention stupid—if you think the sheriff is going to release the man who killed his wife and baby."

"Well, if he don't, he's gonna lose another wife and kid. You just take him the message. Make sure he understands we mean business."

Eleanor beat at his chest, doing her best to claw his eyes.

Fisher grasped her wrists in his cruel fist, pulled her close, and planted a kiss on her lips.

"Ugh!" She struggled, finally managing to get him to release her.

"None of that. Or I'll be coming back to see you in the middle of the night. See if you try and fight me off then."

"You p-pig!" she sputtered. "I'll have you know I sleep with a shotgun handy. Just try it."

"Then go on. Take the message." He shoved her away, spun her around and swatted her behind.

Eleanor gathered her skirts and raced to the stable. Spotting a stable hand, she gasped,

"Quick, saddle my horse."

Sam left the telegraph office and walked next door to the sheriff's office. Out front, the sheriff's brothers were saddling up to ride to the cave the old Tyler gang used for a hideout.

Sam opened the door and walked inside.

"Any word on when the judge will be in town?" Tate asked.

Sam held up the telegram. "Tomorrow's stage. That should put the trial on Saturday." "Good day for a trial. Should be enough men in town to empanel a jury."

"Reckon folks will be eager to serve on this one, considering the circumstances."

"Reckon they will."

The sound of rapid hoofbeats reached Sam's ears. "Someone's riding into town in a big hurry." He strode over to the door and opened it. A pretty little blonde nearly fell off her horse in her hurry to dismount.

"Sheriff! Oh my God, Sheriff!"

Luis Tate sprang to tie up the woman's horse. Nash scrambled to catch the woman as she stumbled onto the boardwalk.

Tate emerged. "Gracious, Miss Ellie. What's wrong?"

"What's left of the old Tyler gang, they've got your wife and baby—Congratulations. I didn't know your baby had been born." She continued rambling, "Anyway, if you don't release my brother, they're going to kill them."

Tate grabbed the young woman's upper arms and shook her. "What kind of hogwash are you spouting? Is this some kind of hoax where you think you can trick me into letting your brother go?"

"No, no. I swear. Dooley Fisher accosted me in the garden this morning and told me to tell you straightaway." She broke into sobs.

Tate's face turned white. "Slow down. Tell me exactly

what he said."

"He grabbed me in the garden and told me you'd lose another wife and kid if you didn't let Arvil go. 'Make sure he knows we mean business.' That's what he said."

Sam's body chilled as if someone had just walked over his grave. "What else did he say?" What about Celine?"

Miss Barnes's brow furrowed. "Who? That's *all* he said."

"He didn't mention anyone else? There was another woman at the sheriff's ranch this morning."

"No."

Had Celine already run away, or was she being held hostage too? And if she was being held hostage, did they know she was a marshal's wife?

"Releasing Barnes is out of the question," Sam said.

"Agreed," the sheriff said with a nod. "There's a trail to the back of the ranch. We'll have to circle around, approach from behind. That might be how they came in. If we can pick up their trail, we can figure out how many gang members there are. Have to be at least two."

Two men, at least, for three hostages: one a baby, plus a woman who'd just given birth. Only Celine was of capable of fighting back. And if she resisted, would this gang of thugs kill her without thinking twice?

Chapter Nine

After proving no additional weapons had been concealed in the sheriff's bedroom, Selma led the way downstairs, O'Reilly on her heels and gripping the shotgun. She found the gang's leader peering out the living room window. "Mr. Hunt, do you honestly believe you're going to get away with holding us hostage? The sheriff and the US marshal will take care of your sorry behinds before you can say 'who was that masked man'."

Hunt snorted. "It's a good thang that other woman ain't as mouthy as you." He crossed the room in long strides, then grabbed her wrist. "Don't know as I could put up with two like you."

"She's just had a baby. She doesn't have the energy to mouth off."

Mad Dog stepped forward. "Now, Booker, don't you be manhandling this lovely lady. Don'cha think she looks all tuckered out, poor soul." He rubbed his groin in a lewd manner. "Want to have a little lie down?"

His gesture and suggestive tone sent Selma's stomach

plummeting to her knees. "No thank you, Mr. O'Reilly." She backed away from him, shivering under his leering gaze. "I'm a married lady."

O'Reilly's gaze went to her left hand. "Where be your weddin' ring, then?"

"She's not married," Hunt interjected. "She's the seamstress. Has a shop in town."

"Now would ye be lyin' to me, darling?"

"We're separated, but..." Should she admit she was the marshal's wife? Would that increase her chances of surviving or lessen them? "The marshal—he's my husband. I left him several years ago, but we've recently been *reunited*." Not exactly reunited, but O'Reilly didn't need to know that.

"So you're of value for more than your glowin' skin and lovely tits." He nodded. "Aye." What could he be thinking? Actually, she didn't want to know what thoughts resided in his crazed mind. His earlier reassurances about his nickname hadn't had the desired effect. To her way of thinking, he was more than a little crazy. In fact, he reminded her of one of her mother's customers who had a tendency to hurt the women he bedded, so much so that her mother finally banned him from the establishment.

The third member of the gang, who'd been missing for a time, burst in through the front door. "There's a wagon heading up the road. Man and woman in it."

"That's probably the Craytons," Selma said. "The sheriff went after Mrs. Crayton—she's a midwife—last night, but she wasn't home. Mr. Crayton must be bringing her over to see if she's still needed."

"Get rid of 'em."

"Yes." Somehow she had to get a message to Sam and

the sheriff about the gang. Hands trembling, she walked over to the door and waited until the wagon approached, then stepped outside.

She pasted a smile on her face. "You're too late. Mrs. Tate has had her baby. They're doing fine."

"I'll be the judge of that." Mrs. Crayton jumped down from the wagon and gathered her bag. "Who delivered the baby? *You?*"

Selma set her hands on her hips. "Yes, as a matter of fact I did."

The rancher's wife sniffed, curling her upper lip. She stepped onto the porch. Selma blocked her way. "I *said* there's nothing for you to do here." She tried to convey with a fearful expression and small movements of her hand for the woman to go away.

"Miss Nelson, what on earth is wrong with your eyes? They're darting all around. You about to have a fit or something?"

The door opened behind Selma, and Hunt shoved her aside. He grabbed Mrs. Crayton's wrist.

"Get the sheriff, Mr. Crayton. Run!" Selma yelled.

Before the rancher could turn the wagon around, Dooley Fisher stepped around the corner of the house and fired a shot at the man. Crayton let out a cry of pain and fell from the seat. The horse startled and thundered away, the wagon rumbling behind.

Mrs. Crayton shrieked, "Tom! You've killed him!" She tried to pull away, but Dooley and Hunt bundled both women back inside the house.

"What's going on here?" The poor woman whipped her head from side to side, her eyes wide with fear and confusion.

Selma slipped her arm around Mrs. Crayton's waist. "Mr. Hunt, Mr. Fisher, and their friend Mr. O'Reilly have taken us prisoner. They want to strike a bargain with the sheriff to release Arvil Barnes before he can go to trial."

Mrs. Crayton's gaze traveled toward the window. "My husband," she wailed. "Please let me see to him."

"No point." Mad Dog strode out the door, letting it slam behind him. Then came the sharp report of gunfire.

Mrs. Crayton flinched, then collapsed into Selma's arms, moaning, "No. Oh no!"

O'Reilly strode back inside. "Now he don't need any seeing to. But if you're of a mind to..."

A loud wail pierced through the house. Mrs. Crayton's jaw tightened. "The babe. May I at least see to the little one?" The woman seemed to gather her wits as well as her strength.

A sense of resignation flashed through Selma. If there was nothing Mrs. Crayton could do for her husband, she might as well make herself useful.

Hunt jerked his head toward the stairs. "Yeah, see to the kid."

Selma breathed a sigh of relief when the woman squared her shoulders and headed for the stairs. "Don't let Star know what just happened. No point in upsetting her further. It's not like she can do anything after just having had a baby."

Someone had to keep a clear head, and it appeared that she was elected. "Have y'all had breakfast?" Maybe she could sneak something into their food that would incapacitate the men.

No. That would only work if she didn't have to eat the food herself or, worse, feed it to Star and Mrs. Crayton.

"No," Hunt said. "We et before we broke camp this morning."

"Now, darlin', ye wouldn't be wantin' to poison us, would ye?" O'Reilly cast a skeptical glance in her direction.

"*Poi-son*?" Her voice broke. How had he divined her intent so quickly? *Who, me*? "No. I just know you're more likely to keep your heads about you if your bellies are full."

O'Reilly sidled up beside her. "And ye bein' so thoughtful. I *like* a thoughtful woman, I do."

Her mouth dried. The thought of O'Reilly touching her was enough to make her want to vomit. "I'm not *that* thoughtful," she said with a touch of heat.

"I'll see just how accommodatin' you are when push comes to shove, me darlin'. I can't imagine what would make a fine woman like yourself run away from her husband, but I can surely see why he would hunt you down." His pale blue gaze traveled to her breasts, lingering several moments too long to suit her, then back up to her face.

Selma clenched her jaw to keep from saying what she really thought. No point in spouting off. Not when she had two other women and a baby to look out for. None of them would present any kind of threat. Poor Betty Crayton was devastated. Just taking care of Star and the baby would likely tax her abilities and strength, but at least it would keep her mind occupied, for the time being anyway, from her grief.

Still, what kind of outcome could this situation have? Neither Sam nor the sheriff would be inclined to give in to the gang's demands. What *would* they do? Most likely they would form a posse and launch some kind of attack. She'd have to prepare the women upstairs for the sound of gunfire. As for herself, she'd have to be ready to help from the inside. But what could she do under the close scrutiny of those miscreants, especially O'Reilly? Of the three men, she found him the most repellent, and the unease she felt when he looked at her...

The sheriff spread a large map of the Texas Hill Country over his desk. "That's the plan. What do you think?"

Sam rubbed his chin and considered the details before nodding his approval. By afternoon, the sheriff had raised a posse of twenty men. Three were to remain with the sheriff's brother Nash at the jail, in case holding the women hostage was a distraction from what was actually a breakout scheme. Luis, being the best tracker within a hundred miles, would meet up with the rest of the posse after he followed the Barnes woman to the sheriff's ranch.

"What about Barnes's sister? Is it possible she's a part of this?" Sam asked.

The sheriff shook his head. "Doubt it. Miss Barnes is a fine young woman. She'll give them the message and leave. I don't want to risk her becoming another one of the hostages. Luis, you follow her and make sure she doesn't."

"Right, then." Sam checked his Colt .45.

After Ellie Barnes had agreed to their scheme and left with Luis, Sam said, "I don't like the thought of leaving our women with these bastards the rest of the day and evening, but it's too risky to attack in daylight. More risk to our womenfolk. I say we strike in the early morning hours when the men will be at their weakest."

"Agreed. By then, Luis will be able be able to tell us

how many there are and how well they're armed. Then we'll meet up where the Pony Creek splits off from the San Saba River."

"This is unfamiliar ground for me, Sheriff. I'd like us to get into place before nightfall."

"Agreed." The sheriff's demeanor was as calm as if this weren't his wife and babe involved. His stony countenance, however, told Sam the young lawman wouldn't put up with any crap from the outlaws. Their fate was sealed.

As for Sam, he couldn't wait to get ahold of the men who'd taken his wife prisoner. If anything happened to her, he'd kill every last one of the bastards.

Luis followed Eleanor Barnes from a mile behind. No point in rushing, since he knew exactly where she was headed. No point in alerting her to his presence either. Whether or not she was in on the scheme, he didn't know. She'd certainly seemed upset enough to be an unwilling pawn. But she might be a damn fine actress too. Most women were.

She'd been instructed to stay mounted and remain far enough away to keep from getting caught, but when he rounded the bend in the road, he spied her slipping off her horse to kneel in the dirt beside what appeared to be a man's body.

Son of a bitch.

They'd shot someone. Was it one of the gang or someone who'd happened to come along at the wrong time?

He slid off his gelding, leaving him tied to a cottonwood, and crept forward, thankful for the thick growth of bluebonnets and Indian blanket. He was close enough to hear her sobs.

Hold it together, Ellie.

Dead man or not, giving them Cord's message was vital to the plan.

The front door opened. Luis ducked down, straining to hear what was said. "Settle down, girl. Ain't ya never seen a dead man before?"

Luis didn't recognize the voice or the shotgun-toting, ginger-haired man.

Ellie stood, backing away as soon as she could steady herself. "I've a message from the sheriff. He'll let Arvil go in the morning, early, while the town's asleep and don't know what's going on."

"Just like that he's going to let the man go who killed his wife?"

Ellie nodded. "He wasn't happy, but he doesn't want anything to happen to this wife and baby."

"Smart man. Now, what about that marshal? I don't reckon he'd be in favor of lettin' the man go either. Of course, we be havin' his wife too." The man's low, sinister laugh chilled Luis to his bones.

"I don't understand how—"

"Don't have to, darlin'."

The stranger was joined on the porch by someone Luis knew: Booker Hunt, one of the Tyler gang. "And just how is Arvil supposed to get out here?"

"The sheriff will give him a horse and instruct him to ride here. You'll leave then—right?"

"We may need to take one of the women with us, just to make sure we're not followed. Tell the marshal we'll take good care of her."

"Aye," the Irishman said. "Indeed we will."

Luis lay still in the field of wildflowers until Ellie had remounted and headed back to town. Nothing he could do for the man lying in the dirt. He waited until both Hunt and the Irishman had gone back inside the house before creeping his way back to his gelding. Mounting, he then spurred the gelding to a gentle trot, and under cover of the thick cottonwoods, he headed back to town. His reconnaissance had gained valuable information. Three men held the women hostage, and at least one of them was a stone-cold killer.

Upstairs in the bedroom, Selma knelt beside Mrs. Crayton, doing her best to calm the new widow, who sobbed and raged by turns. "You've got to control yourself," she said. "These men will get rid of anyone they think is more trouble than they're worth. If we live through this, you'll have the rest of your life to grieve for your husband. But for now, you have to concentrate on helping me care for Star and her baby."

"You're a fine one to be giving folks orders, *Miss* Nelson. You don't have a husband who was just shot before your very eyes!" Mrs. Crayton fisted her hands in her skirts.

"I'm the only one with a clear head, Betty. Star just had a baby. She can't be expected to get up and do anything to free us. The way to survive is to keep calm. You *need* to keep your head down and stay out of sight."

"I'm so sorry," Star murmured from the bed, clutching

the baby to her breast.

"But they just murdered my husband," Mrs. Crayton wailed.

"I know." Selma hugged her. "I'm so sorry."

The woman wrung her hands. "He's just a-lying out there in the road like he was an animal. It ain't fittin' such a good man be treated like that."

"I know. I know." She patted Mrs. Crayton's shoulder. Not even when delivering Star's baby had she felt as useless as she did now, confronting this woman's grief. "I'll try talking them into letting me move him to the ice house."

"He was a *good man*."

"And you're a strong woman. You can bear this. You have to."

Betty Crayton shook her head, but her sobs quieted until she squared her shoulders and met Selma's gaze. "Sorry. It was such a shock, seeing him shot like that."

"If you can just help with caring for Star, maybe I'll be able to keep these scoundrels placated."

"Don't trust any of 'em," Star warned. "That Irishman has a bad look about him. The way his eyes..."

Selma nodded. "He's a concern, but I have a plan." If she could just turn them on each other, she might be able to take care of the last one with the six-shooter she'd packed into her sewing basket. Now just how would she go about it?

As Selma made her way downstairs, she divined the perfect solution to turn the men against each other. But first, she'd keep her promise to Mrs. Crayton about moving her husband's body.

Selma found Booker Hunt where he peered through one of the parlor windows.

"Mr. Hunt, would it be possible for one of your men to help me move Mr. Crayton's body to the ice house? His wife is understandably upset."

Hunt nodded. "Dooley, you give her a hand. Mind you, Miss Nelson, no funny business."

"Nothing funny about our friend and neighbor being killed like a dog and left lying in the dirt."

"'Twas necessary."

"So you say. But I say it's necessary to treat the man with some dignity until..."

"Until you're rescued. That's what you think is going to happen?"

"I don't know what's going to happen, sir, but he shouldn't be left in the road like that."

"Go on, then. Suit yourself." He jerked his head at Dooley. "Go on. Be quick about it."

"Thank you, Mr. Hunt. I'm sure his widow appreciates this small kindness."

Very small kindness indeed.

After Mr. Crayton had been conveyed to the ice house and his widow apprised of the same, Selma picked up the egg basket from the kitchen and walked into the parlor. "May I gather the eggs? You'll want them in the morning if you're still here."

"I'll be going with ye." The Irishman's expression perked up. "No tellin' what kind of weapons ye'll find."

She arched a brow. "In the henhouse? Really?"

"I don't trust ye—not after the stunt ye pulled with the shotgun."

"Fine. Be my guest." She sauntered outside as if she

hadn't a care in the world.

Hook.

On the way to the henhouse, she asked, "So, how did you get mixed up with Mr. Hunt and Mr. Dooley?"

O'Reilly shrugged. "Said they needed a third man on a job."

She smiled sweetly. "So you helped them kidnap three women and a baby out of the goodness of your heart?"

"Do I look barmy? O'course they're payin' me."

"Oh...from the bank robbery money?"

Line.

"What bank robbery?"

"Three years ago, the one where they killed the sheriff's first wife."

"They said all that money was gone."

She stopped and graced him with her most incredulous expression. "Are you serious? They told you the money was all gone? Mercy me, I don't see how they could've spent that much money in thirty years—much less three. Not with all the gold they stole."

And sinker.

"Gold?" His pale blue gaze widened. "Bastards never said nothin' about any gold."

He spun on his heel, storming back to the house. She followed. Surely in the ensuing ruckus she could get to her sewing basket and the hidden six-shooter.

Chapter Ten

At the point where Pony Creek split off from the San Saba River, Sam waited with the rest of the posse under the cover of cottonwoods and burr oak for Luis Tate to join them. By now, the sheriff's younger brother would've seen how matters stood at the Tate ranch.

"You're sure he's as good as you say?" Sam asked. "We've a lot to lose if he's been caught. We'd have to go in blind."

Sheriff Tate gave a snort. "Luis can move through the woods without making a sound. You'd think he was part redskin. He can track anything on two or four feet. When Tommy Tyler kidnapped my wife, Luis followed the trail all the way to outside Austin."

"You all talking about me?"

Startled, Sam glanced over his shoulder. Luis had come up behind them without making a sound. And on horseback at that. "Reckon you deserve your reputation." Sam tipped his hat, acknowledging his admiration.

"Three men," Luis said, "and they've killed someone. There's a man lying in the road."

Sam listened intently as the deputy spoke. Every bit of information the deputy gleaned was important. "Could you see who they were?"

"Just like we thought—what's left of the Tyler gang, Booker Hunt and Dooley Fisher. There's a third man, one I didn't recognize."

Sam straightened in the saddle. "Describe him."

"My height, ginger-red hair. Spoke with an Irish brogue."

"An Irishman?" Sam shook his head. "Only one I know is Mad Dog O'Reilly. He's a bad character. Haven't come across many worse."

"How so?" The sheriff shifted in the saddle.

"Might not be the same one. Last information the marshal's office had stated he might be headed this way. Better hope it's not. He's an expert with explosives, and he's wanted for killing two women in the Arizona territory. After he has his way with 'em, he butchers 'em like cattle."

Tate's eyes widened. "We've got to get them out of there." He pulled on the reins, obviously ready to head home.

Sam wheeled his horse around and grabbed the bridle of Tate's horse. "Hold on now. Rushing in unprepared is likely to get them killed."

Tate bristled. "I'm not about to lose another wife and baby to this bunch."

"Gotta stick to the plan. Only way. We'll ride as soon as the sun goes down. Under cover of darkness, we'll approach and wait."

"But my family..." The sheriff gulped, his desperation written plainly across his face.

"My wife's in there too."

"But you..."

"She's still my wife," Sam said under his breath. Not necessary for the rest of the posse to know Miss Nelson was his wife, nor just how much he still cared.

"There's more," Luis said. "When I caught up with Ellie Barnes, she told me the dead man was Bob Crayton."

"Shit." The sheriff paled. "He was going to bring his wife over when she returned home." "Three women and a baby held hostage." Could things get any worse?

Selma inched her way toward her sewing basket in the corner. Better to keep out of the line of fire. And get closer to her six-shooter.

"You thought you could hire me for a few lousy dollars when all the time you have a stash of gold hidden away? I want a share of what's left if you expect me to stay here and deal with these women."

"Deal with these women?" What did O'Reilly mean by that? Whatever he meant, it didn't sound good.

"Gold? There ain't no damn gold," Booker Hunt sputtered, his face growing red with rage.

"Yeah," Fisher piped in. "Whatever gave you that idea? We only got away with four hundred dollars. After a week in Frisco, that money's long gone."

O'Reilly jerked his head in Selma's direction. "She said you had gold stashed away."

"It's true," Selma insisted, continuing to brazen the lie, grateful an outlaw like O'Reilly was just greedy enough to believe her. Given that he was new to the gang, she prayed that she could undermine his trust, if indeed any had developed. To make it more convincing, she added, "The stage had just delivered it to the bank. The gold was headed from San Antonio to Fort Concho to pay soldiers' salaries. It was one of the last gold deliveries made before the fort closed last year."

"She's out of her ever-loving mind," Hunt said, his face growing even redder, his hand hovering near his weapon. "There warn't no gold. Never."

"Yer lyin'!" O'Reilly's hand rested on the butt of his gun. "I'll be having a third of it. Now tell me where 'tis?" Squaring his shoulders, he planted his feet apart.

Selma ducked behind the settee, just inches from her sewing basket. Oh Lord, her plan was actually going to work.

Peeking over the back of the settee, she saw Hunt grab his gun, but O'Reilly beat him to the draw, shooting Hunt squarely in the chest with what was likely a mortal wound.

From the other side of the room, Fisher drew a second later, hitting O'Reilly in the side. "Bastard!" O'Reilly spun, firing once more, hitting Fisher right between the eyes.

Two down and one to go.

Selma slipped her hand inside the sewing basket and pulled out her six-shooter, aiming it at O'Reilly's back. "Put down your weapon, Mr. O'Reilly. So help me, I'll shoot."

O'Reilly spun, his eyes widening, then narrowing. "Oh ye will, will ye?" He closed the distance between them in two limping strides.

Her hand and arm trembled with the weight of the gun. Dear Lord, could she shoot this man? Or any man?

"What's going on down there?" Mrs. Crayton called from the stairway. Selma glanced toward the stairs, her attention wavering for a second.

Still grabbing his flank with one hand, O'Reilly knocked the gun from her grip, relieving her of ever knowing the answer to her question.

"Stupid whore." He raised his arm as if to backhand her.

She jumped back out of his reach. "I may be stupid, but you're the one who's bleeding." He opened his shirt and glanced at his wound. "'Tis nothin'. Flesh wound."

"Even so, you're bleeding, and you need a bandage," she said, praying to buy them some time. "Mrs. Crayton, please go back upstairs and bring me some clean linens. I'll dress his wound." She cast him a wary look. "Then you can go find the gold." Star and Mrs. Crayton wouldn't be safe until she could get him out of the house.

She walked over to Booker Hunt and knelt beside him. His breath came in ragged gasps, blood frothing from his mouth. "I'm sorry," she said. "I didn't have a choice."

"The gold..." Hunt shuddered, then died.

O'Reilly jerked her to her feet. "Ye better be tellin' me true. Is there any gold? Blast ye! Tell me the truth!"

"But there is...truly. You heard him. He mentioned the gold with his dying breath." Her voice wavered, but she persevered. "And I know where they might've hidden it." If she could send him on a wild-goose chase, then she could ride for help. "I can draw you a map." "Won't be needin' a map, darlin'. Ye'll take me to it. And just so ye know, I don't take well to bein' disappointed."

Damnation. That wasn't part of her plan.

While they waited for time to pass before they could surround the sheriff's ranch house, the posse set up a makeshift camp beneath the broad canopy of an ancient cottonwood. Sam leaned against the tree's gnarled trunk, turning his Stetson in his hands. Waiting, when every bone in his body urged him to rush in and free Celine and the other women, had him on edge. The sheriff too, apparently. He paced from one side of the camp to the other.

"Tate," Sam said, "sit and stay awhile. You oughta be getting some shut-eye."

"Can't. No telling what's going on inside my home. That's my wife and son in there." He ran a hand through his hair, then reseated his Stetson.

Luis stepped forward. "Let me go."

"There's not enough cover between here and the house, even for you," his brother replied.

"The sun will be behind the hills. I'll go in then. There's only a mile to cover before I reach the outbuildings. I can do it. We need to know what's going on inside that house beforehand."

The sheriff cut his gaze toward Sam. "What do you think?"

"He's *your* brother. If you think he can get close enough, I say let 'em try.

"Dusk it is, then." Luis settled down on his bedroll and appeared to go to sleep. Sam frowned. "How does he do that?"

"Beats me," Tate said. "He and Nash are twins, but you'd never know they came from the same ma. When we were kids, we used to tell 'im that he was a changeling."

Smiling, Sam hunkered down and checked his revolver. "Just want all you men to remember we have three women and a baby in that house. Make each shot count. Waiting ain't easy, but that's what we have to do. Get some rest. We need to be wide awake when this gang is asleep and comfortable. They won't be expecting us. Two of em you know. Booker Hunt and Dooley Fisher. Wild card is this Irish fella. If he's who I think he is, he's the one who'll give us the most trouble."

Luis sat up, then sprang to his feet. "Gunfire. Three shots."

Three shots. Three women.

Panic squeezed Sam's heart, but he forced himself to remain calm, at least on the outside.

The sheriff eyeballed Sam. "No point in waiting now."

"Agreed. Let's ride."

O'Reilly sat with his gun trained on Selma while she rapidly dressed his flesh wound. "There," she said, tucking in the edge of the bandage.

He raised his arm, twisting around to check her efforts. "Nice job. Good as any sawbones."

If only she could've added some manure or some other noxious substance into the ointment, but he'd watched her too carefully. "I'm so glad you approve, Mr. O'Reilly."

He got to his feet, then grabbed her wrist. "Now,

take me to the gold. If yer lyin', it'll be the last lie ye ever tell."

She could well believe his words. No matter what he did to her, at least by his taking her to search for the nonexistent gold, the other women would have a chance at being rescued. "May I tell my friends where we're going?"

"No. Let's get goin'."

"I *have* to tell them good-bye so they won't worry."

"No!" His hand rested ominously on his gun. "And if there's no gold, I'll be comin' back to kill them all."

Her heart sank. There went all her hopes of ensuring her friends' survival. Not only was there no gold, she didn't know anything about the countryside, much less where the reputed hideout cave was. If she could just lead him around long enough, surely, Sam and the sheriff would return to the ranch as soon as Ellie Barnes's message was delivered. Whatever O'Reilly did to her would be worth saving her friends.

"May I change into something more suitable for a long ride?"

"What ye've got on will do."

"May we, at least, go in my buggy? I'm not accustomed to riding astride, certainly not for long distances."

"No changin' clothes. No buggy! Get your arse a-movin' before I lose me patience."

"But—"

"Forget it. There's no time."

With that, he yanked her outside. Dusk would soon fall. Perhaps she could escape, steal away and hide in the darkness.

He whipped out a rope, then tied her hands behind her. "You expect me to ride without using my hands?"

"I'll lead yer horse by its tether. All ye have to do is tell me which way to the gold."

Within minutes of hearing the shots, Sam and the sheriff had concealed themselves in front of the ranch house, the rest of the posse taking positions around it. "You're surrounded," Sam yelled. "Come on out with your hands up."

No response. At least the gang wasn't stupid enough to try to shoot their way out. Sam nodded, giving Tate the go-ahead to enter the house.

The sheriff breached the door first. "Hunt and Fisher dead," he called out. Sam followed the sheriff.

Crayton's widow, Sam assumed, met them at the foot of the stairs. "Your wife and son are all right," she said, her face pale and drawn.

Tate bounded upstairs with Sam on his heels. They burst through the bedroom door.

Relief washed over him. With a worried expression, the sheriff's wife was sitting up in bed, clutching their babe. Tate sank to his knees beside Star's bed. "Thank God you're all right."

"He took Selma with him," Star said. "We heard the gunfire, then Mrs. Crayton saw them ride off. He'd tied Selma's hands behind her back, and he was leading her on one of their horses."

"The Irishman?" Sam asked.

"Yes. How did you know he was Irish?"

"Never mind that now." The rotten bastard had taken Celine. Why would he? A woman would just slow him down. Then a sickening sensation staggered him. He reached for the doorjamb to steady himself. Without a doubt, the Irishman would have his way with her before he carved her up.

For once, it didn't matter that she'd stolen Sam's life savings. He couldn't let something like that happen to the woman he loved.

Yes, dammit. He still loved her. No matter how he'd tried to deny it, seeing her again after three long years had reminded him of the passion they'd shared, and, more importantly, it had reawakened the tenderness, robbing him of his determination to see her face justice.

Chapter Eleven

The rays of the April sun beamed down as hot as any in July. Perspiration beaded on Selma's forehead and collected between her shoulders. They'd been heading into the hills east of the ranch for at least half an hour. Her mouth had grown dryer than cotton. "I'm thirsty."

"Ye'll get some water when we reach this hideout cave. How much farther?"

If she only knew. From what little she remembered about Star's stories about her late brother, the cave was located somewhere in the hills beyond the Tyler ranch. "I think we need to head more eastward," she said. "Toward the old San Saba silver mines." Whether those mines ever existed at all or were mere the stuff of legend was the question.

"I've heard of 'em but thought they weren't real."

"Oh, they're real, all right. But I'm not a native Texan, so I'm a little fuzzy on their exact whereabouts."

"Fuzzy, are ye?" O'Reilly whipped around in this saddle. "Ye have to do better than that, darlin'."

His gaze focused on her breasts, unnerving her. Not to mention there was something terribly unsettling in the way his lips twitched when he looked at her. "I'm sure the cave is close, just higher into the hills." Their actual chances of stumbling across the hideout cave— or any cave—were close to nil, but she had to brazen it out, no matter what happened. The farther she drew him away from the sheriff's ranch, the better.

"How far be the *bleedin'* cave?" he asked, apparently losing whatever passed for patience in his crazed mind.

"From what Mrs. Tate—she was Bobby Tyler's half-sister—told me, it might take us another hour." O'Reilly spurred his horse, resulting in her nearly falling off her mount. "Not so fast. Are you trying to kill me in the process?"

He pulled back on the reins, slowing the pace. "Now that would be a downright shame, because once we find that gold, I intend to show ye what a real man does with a woman. I be guessin' that ye haven't had a hard ride in quite a spell."

A cold chill slid down her back. "Such talk is hardly appropriate, Mr. O'Reilly." If she had to, she'd survive his manhandling or worse, as long as it kept him away from the ranch and her friends.

Besides, Sam would come looking for her. Yes, he would.

Sam rode apace with the sheriff's deputy as they followed the clear trail the Irishman and Celine had taken from the sheriff's ranch. The sheriff and two of the posse had stayed behind to search the rest of the outbuildings.

"Where in the hell is he taking her?" Sam asked aloud.

"Tracks lead into the hills-not the path I would've picked to get the hell out of Dodge. Two horses, moving at a decent pace." Luis leaned forward in his saddle. "If he's tied her hands, that'll slow him down some."

"Why would he take her? As you said, she'll slow him down."

Luis swept off his Stetson and wiped his forehead with a bandanna. "Must've thought there was some advantage to keeping her other than as a hostage."

"I've heard what he does to women," Sam said, repressing a shudder. "But Celine's a strong woman—"

"Celine?" Luis frowned. "I thought we were talking about Miss Nelson."

"Selma Nelson is really Celine Boudreau...Dunaway, my wife," he told the deputy.

"Oh," Luis replied, his gaze widening. "Now that makes all this a mite more interesting." "Don't it, though."

Luis slipped from his mount, knelt down, placed his ear to the ground and listened. Then, getting to his feet, he said, "We aren't too far behind. Shouldn't take too long to catch up to 'em."

Behind him, Sam heard the sound of a horseman approaching. He twisted around in his saddle to have a look. The sheriff joined Sam and Luis at the head of the posse. "'I left two men back at the ranch to guard the women," he said.

"Good idea," Sam said. "Couldn't have been easy leaving your wife."

"It's my place to be here. I want that Irishman almost as bad as you do."

"I doubt he's gonna need a trial, though."

"Strikes me as the kind who'll fight to the finish." Sam smiled, relishing that exact outcome. "Hope so."

*

Selma's thighs ached from the unaccustomed exertions of riding a horse over the Hill Country terrain. A slight but welcome breeze rustled through the scattered growth of cottonwoods. Perspiration mixed with trail dust left dirty rivulets down her garment, causing her to wonder just how bad she must smell.

"How much farther is this bloody cave?" O'Reilly asked over his shoulder.

"I believe it's over the next ridge...in the next valley." If only that were true.

The Irishman glanced over his shoulder. "Don't ye know for sure?"

"Not exactly." Needless to say, and even more important not to say, she didn't know where the hell she was. She supposed they were still in Texas.

"And ye were going to draw me a bleedin' map?"

"That might've been a bit of an exaggeration," she admitted.

"I'll show ye exaggeratin'." He jerked on her mount's lead, nearly unseating her again.

"Damnation! Unlike most of the people around here, I wasn't born in the saddle. If you do that again, I'll fall and be no use to you at all."

"Ye're precious little use to me now. Bleedin' damn woman. Ye lied. Admit it!"

"Yes!" she hissed. "I might've lied about knowing *exactly* where it was, but it's rumored to be in these hills. If we keep going, we'll find it. She gripped the horse's sides with her knees. "At least tie my hands in front so I can hold on as we go over this next ridge."

O'Reilly pulled off his cowboy hat, then mopped his face with his neckerchief. "Jaysusl I be hatin' this heat. It's only bleedin' April."

"Then maybe you should've stayed in the home country. It must be cooler there. What's it like?"

"Greener-than-green hills as far as the eye can see. Stone outcrops. Stone fence rows creating a patchwork like ye've never seen." His tone grew almost lyrical as he described his country.

"Then why did you leave?" More than likely he'd killed someone, but she had to keep him talking, keep his mind off the gold he wouldn't find even if they found a cave.

"Ah, well, there was a bit of unpleasantness. Me da was a hard man. He hated me guts, to put it mildly. Considered me an ungrateful whelp—aye, that's what he called me."

"What happened?"

"One night after he broke me ma's jaw—for the second time, mind ye—I stove his head in while he slept. With a price on me head, I made my way toward the coast to Dublin. Stowed away aboard a ship. Nearly starved on that voyage, but I made it to America."

"You were free."

"Free to starve...or make my way the best I could."

"I see." So robbery and murder was how he'd made his way. No telling what else he'd done.

"What about ye?'"

"Me?" The man actually wanted to converse. Good. "I grew up in New Orleans. After my mother died, I came west with a bit of inheritance and set up my dry-goods-and-dressmaking shop." No point in telling him the full story. None at all.

"When did ye marry the marshal?"

"That was a bit of a side trip before I settled in Kenton Valley." She kept talking, anything to keep his mind off the gold and her body, but from his frequent leering gazes, she wasn't having much success.

They began to climb, the horses struggling in the rough terrain. In order to remain seated and maintain her balance, she leaned low over the saddle horn. "Why can't you just tie my hands in front? Riding would be so much easier."

"Shut your cakehole. I'll not be tyin' yer bleeding' hands round the front. Some sort of fool ye must think I am."

"Not at all. It's just as I've already told you, I'm not used to riding horseback, much less *astride*."

He whipped around again at the word astride. His upper lip lifted in a sneer. "Ye'll find a harder mount to ride afore this day is over. Consider this part of yer breakin' in."

In spite of the warmth of the day, goose bumps covered her arms. Without a doubt, the Irishman intended to force himself on her—unless Sam could stop him. And would Sam even try? Surely, he'd find them soon. A surge of hope rose in her breast, even as she blinked back the tears. Maybe her husband was already on their trail. No matter how angry he was with her, he wouldn't want her ravaged, savaged or worse. And when O'Reilly ultimately discovered she'd lied about the gold, he'd kill her for sure.

Chapter Twelve

The sun was starting to dip below the next ridge of mountains. For several hours, the posse had ridden in silence, each man keeping his own counsel. "Where the hell is he taking her?" Sam asked, for a moment not realizing he'd spoken aloud.

Ahead of him, Luis slowed the pace and shrugged. "They're headed into the mountains. Lots of caves where he can hide for days—like the Tyler gang's old hideout."

Riding beside Sam, the sheriff shook his head. "How in blue blazes would the Irishman know where that cave is? He wasn't a part of Tyler's gang. Appears he's a gun for hire that they took on to increase their odds at breaking out Barnes."

A cave where the Irishman could hold out for days and do whatever the hell he wanted to Celine. Not if Sam had any say in the matter. He'd cut the bastard's throat if he so much as touched Celine's silken skin. As he rode, dark visions filled his mind with all the things he'd do to O'Reilly if the outlaw more than touched her.

"Since he's a stranger to these parts, he'll need to make camp before dark," Luis said. Sam squinted into the sun. "How far do you think we're behind 'em?"

"Less than an hour's ride." Luis peered ahead, shading his eyes. "Can't risk getting too close too soon, or he'll see us."

"Can't risk him holin' up in a cave after dark with my wife either." Sam spurred his gelding. "Let's move."

After a tricky and frequently perilous descent to the valley floor, Selma let out a sigh of relief. It was a complete miracle she hadn't fallen and rolled across scraggly brush and loose rocks all the way to the bottom.

Never, she swore, would she ever get on another horse. Every muscle in her body ached from long hours in the saddle. The sun was a bit lower in the sky, but nighttime in these hills could turn cool, no matter how warm the day had been.

"Aren't we going to stop for the night?" Though she tried, she couldn't keep the whine from her voice and sounded like a plaintive child.

"Yer the one what's supposed to know. How much farther?"

"Damned if I know," she said, exasperation getting the better of her. Where the hell was her husband? Surely he'd cared enough to form a posse to chase down this outlaw. No, he'd probably wiped his hands of her, saying good riddance to bad rubbish. Tears started to form, threatening to spill down her cheeks.

Her stomach growled. "Did you think to bring something to eat? I'm starving."

"Damme if yer not the complainin'est women I ever saw. Shut your cakehole. I've had enough of your whinin' and moanin' and groanin'."

"You didn't, did you? Well, you're welcome to starve."

She straightened in the saddle and peered over his shoulder for the sign of a cave up ahead. At this point, any cave would do. No matter what depravity awaited her.

"Look!" She would've jumped up and down for joy if she hadn't been on horseback.

"There it is—a cave. It has to be the one."

"So ye say. I be thinkin' right about now ye'd say just about anythin'."

"Please, can't we just stop? It'll be dark soon enough. You don't know your way around these hills, and neither do I...in the dark, anyway." She tacked on the last bit to keep him from thinking she was completely useless and worthy of being discarded.

"I sees it. All right. Reckon yer marshal don't care enough to come after ye." His tone held a note of glee.

"Well, if he does come after me, you're a dead man."

"We be seein' about that, missus."

Picking their way through the rugged terrain, they reached the cave's entrance. He swung a leg over his horse, dismounting easily, then pulled a long knife from the leather sheath on his belt. He walked toward her, the blade reflecting the orange sky at sunset. Selma sucked in a deep breath. Was he going to kill her after all?

At the top of the mountain ridge, Sam and the rest of the posse gazed down into the valley, looking for any trace of the Irishman and Celine.

"There's a cave not too far along this valley," Luis said. "Gold miners tried mining it, but it never panned out much more than a little gold dust. I'll scout ahead to see if they've taken shelter for the night."

The sheriff nodded. "One man won't make as much noise as a whole posse. Better chance of taking him by surprise."

Sam knew they were right, but an uneasy feeling in the pit of his gut argued otherwise.

"I'm going with you. That's my wife he's got."

Luis motioned for Sam to follow. "Easy enough trail. Not taking care about the signs he leaves behind."

"He doesn't have to be careful. He's got a hostage."

Selma's gaze focused on O'Reilly. As he walked toward her, his tread was slow, measured as if he were leading a funeral procession. Hers?

At least they'd run across a cave. What he'd do when he discovered there wasn't any gold hidden away, only heaven knew.

O'Reilly led their horses into the cave. *Dammit, Sam, where are you?* She shivered in the cool darkness of the cave. True, there was evidence it had been mined at some time, but did it contain gold from a bank robbery? No.

Without warning, he jerked her from the horse. She fell to the ground, then struggled to her knees.

"That's far enough. It strikes me that a woman such as yerself may be needin' to learn her proper place. To my way d thinking, on yer knees is right where ye belong."

Her jaw clenched. He passed behind her. She strained to keep an eye on him. Was he going to cut her throat? Was this how she would die? Alone? Lying on the hard-packed floor of a cave?

A hard chill shook her entire body. She squared her

shoulders. Fine, just make it quick, she prayed.

Sam followed the deputy. The mouth of the cave was in sight. Luis held a finger to his lips, then nodded.

Sam dragged in a ragged breath of relief. They'd found them. But was Celine still alive? Luis motioned, indicating Sam should return for the rest of the posse. He shook his head. No way was he leaving, not when she was so close.

He pointed at the deputy. *You*, he mouthed. *You bring the rest of em.*

The deputy nodded resignedly and left Sam alone.

No point in having a witness to what was surely going to happen to the Irishman. By the time the posse returned, he'd have Celine in his arms and the Irishman would be dead. At least that was what he hoped.

As soon as Luis slithered away through the brush, Sam moved closer to the cave opening. First, he had to know if Celine was all right.

O'Reilly grabbed Selma's wrists and sliced the rope binding them. She brought her numbed hands around. Her shoulders cramped from having her hands tied behind for so long. She rubbed the raw places where the rope had dug into her skin. "Water," she croaked. "I need water and bandages."

"Ye be thinkin' I'm a bleedin' nursemaid?" He gave a rude snort of a laugh. "Now where's the bloody gold ye told me about?"

"Do I look like a miner? I'm sure they didn't just leave it lying around for anyone to find. It'll be hidden. You'll have to find it"

He pointed at her. "Fine. Start lookin'."

"Me?"

"Yeah, unless ye be wantin' to put yer purty mouth on my cock just to pass the time. First, find the damned gold. Meanwhile, I'll be thinkin' of just how I want ye to pleasure me once ye've found it."

At the thought of his touching her, bile, bitter and vile, rose in the back of her throat. She'd die before touching him anywhere with any part of her person.

And while she was rummaging through a cave filled with all sorts of rock, rubble and stones, she could pick up a good-size rock and secrete it in the pocket of her shirtwaist. Such a stone would do nicely to bash his head in, given the opportunity of course.

"We really should build a fire first. It's going to get cold once the sun goes down."

"Don't be worryin' yer pretty head 'bout that. There's ways of keepin' warm that don't require a fire."

She restrained the trembling that threatened to convulse her body. If all she had to fight with her were hands and nails, she'd scratch his eyes out before she'd let him touch her.

"Fine. I'll look for the damned gold, but it's really dark back here. Can't you at least rig up some kind of a torch? This cave seems pretty deep. There may be passages off the main cave that go on for miles. I can hardly find the gold if it's stashed away in one of those, can I?"

He shrugged. "Ye might be having a point there, darlin'."

*

Sam tied his horse to a bush, then crept toward the cave entrance. Close enough he should be able to hear their voices. He could just make out the low, muttering tones of a man. The Irishman, of course.

Bastard better not have hurt Celine. Whatever'd happened, it was time the Irish outlaw got a taste of justice—Texas style. Maybe not the kind a judge would approve of, but the kind any man in the posse would mete out to someone who hurt the woman he loved.

Yes, dammit, he still loved Celine. No matter what she'd done or why she'd done it. That was why seeing her at first had pained him so. With every glance she shot in his direction, she'd cut his heart to shreds.

Could he turn his back on everything he believed in and forgive her? Once he'd sworn he'd see her jailed for her thieving ways. Now, all he wanted was to wrap his arms around her and love her every which way till Sunday.

He kept to the side of the opening, flattening his body against the sheer limestone rock face.

Damn. No longer could he hear the Irishman muttering. Sam eased inside, still keeping against the wall and away from the opening. Two horses were tied in the far side of the cave. One of them nickered softly when it caught his scent.

He froze. He drew his Colt .45 from the holster and eased forward another step, dislodging a loose rock.

Damn. His body tensed, his muscles quivering with the need to find Celine.

A movement of air warned him. Too late. A hand wielding a gun butt whipped through the air and struck his temple.

A shower of stars. Then black. The cave floor careened

upward to smack him in the face.

Selma gripped the torch O'Reilly had found and lit, apparently discarded years ago by the previous inhabitants of the cave. It provided barely enough light to keep her from running into the walls, but at least she could make her way toward the back of the cave.

She stopped and pondered which offshoot to take when a groan echoed throughout the cave. She whipped around.

Sam? He'd come for her after all. Forgetting all pretense of finding the nonexistent gold, she rushed toward the front of the cave. "Sam!"

In the feeble light cast by the torch, she spotted him lying facedown a few feet inside the cave...and O'Reilly squatting beside Sam's still form.

"Damn you! What have you done?"

"A little love tap, me darlin'. That's all I gave him."

"He's hurt." She rushed to Sam's side-or tried to, but the outlaw shoved her away.

"Keep yer bleedin' hands off him. Such a sad sight to behold, he is."

"You've *killed* him." Her heart thundered. No, he couldn't be dead. Please no.

O'Reilly shrugged. "Mebbe. Mebbe not. Just need to keep him out of me way." In the dim light, he squinted up at her. "Did ye find any gold?"

She shook her head. "Not yet. I just barely got started. There are at least three passages left to explore, and this torch is about played out."

Neither his expression nor tone held a drop of

sympathy. "Better get busy, then."

Had Sam come alone? Doubtful. There had to be a posse nearby. If she could play for time until the rest showed up...

But Sam was bleeding from a head wound, and he wasn't coming around. More than anything, she wanted to tend to his injury. She took a tentative step toward his still form.

"I said get busy lookin' for that gold. Otherwise, I'll just shoot him so ye won't be distracted."

"There isn't any *damned* gold," she yelled. "I made that up just to get you away from the ranch."

"Stupid whore!" O'Reilly gave her the back of his hand. Her head rang and stars danced before her eyes while she tried to stand her ground, keeping her feet firmly planted.

His second blow landed squarely on her chin and it was lights-out.

When Selma regained consciousness, she lay next to Sam, her hands bound in front. "Sam?"

He emitted an unintelligible groan. "What?" He grunted, twisting around in an attempt to sit.

"Careful," she warned. "We're in the cave. I don't know where O'Reilly is, but I can hear him moving around."

Rolling over on her side, she tried to sit. "You're not going to get away with this, you know," she shouted.

"Oh, am I not? I be thinkin' I've already gotten away with it. I'll be laughin' all the way to Oklahoma. But ye won't be laughin' long at all. Not once I get this fuse lit."

"Fuse?"

"Ye see, the reason I be recruited to the gang is me

handy way with explosives. Me job was to blow out a wall in the jail to free the prisoner. Poor sod. Guess when all be said and done, he'll stand trial and hang after all."

"So why don't you just hightail it to Oklahoma and leave us be?"

"'Cause I be havin' all this nice dynamite. Hate for it go to waste, ye see."

"Roll toward the wall," Sam whispered. "Get as close as you can. I'll cover your body with mine."

"It won't do any good."

"It's our only hope."

Selma half rolled, half scooted along the floor the short distance to the cave wall, the sharp edges of rock scraping through the thin material of her dress. "It's not going to work."

"Shut the hell up, Celine. Keep moving."

"Bye now," O'Reilly said with an inordinate amount of glee in his tone. "Sweet dreams." The killer led both horses from the cave.

Thoughtful of him.

Returning to the mouth of the cave, O'Reilly struck a lucifer against the cave wall, and after that, all she heard was the inexorable hiss as the flame slithered its way along the fuse.

How long did they have? Not long enough, anyway. "Sam, I'm so sorry. I never should've taken your money, but I had a good reason. At least I thought so at the time."

"Don't matter now, Celine." He rolled, positioning his body over hers. Not that his body could do damn-all to protect her when tons of rock caved in on top of them.

The flame hit the dynamite, the sound deafening. The ground shook, rumbled, and rock rained down.

"I love you, Celine."

Cord nodded, listening carefully while his brother spoke low. Sound could be tricky in these hills and valleys. "The Irishman is holed up in that cave. Sam stayed—can't say as I blame him."

"What about his wife?"

"Saw sign of both horses' tracks leading inside the cave. No sign of her, though. We need to descend as quietly as possible," Luis said to the rest of the posse. "The farther we are from the cave when we go down, the better. Less chance of being heard."

"There's another trail down, about a half mile from here," Cord said. "Will that do?"

Luis nodded. "Less chance of sound carrying from there."

"We've got the bastard outnumbered." Cord swung his gelding around. "Let's ride."

Before Cord and the posse had gone fifty yards, the ground rumbled and shook. Below them, debris and dust belched from the mouth of the cave. "Son of a bitch. He's blown up the cave."

Chapter Thirteen

Would Sam's sweet words be the last she ever heard? Celine huddled in his protective embrace in the blackest night. Coughing, she brushed the dust and dirt from her face, then shook her head. "Sam? Are you all right?" she asked, fearful he wouldn't respond. His body moved ever so slightly. His shoulders twitched as if he were trying to eke out more room. "Sam?"

A low groan emitted from him, a cough, then his breathless reply: "Yeah."

"We're still alive," she said, difficult to believe as it was.

"Barely." He gave a cough. "If you consider we're buried alive under tons of rock." "There must be some air, or we wouldn't be talking. Are you hurt?"

"Something's poking my back. Can't feel my legs. Ribs hurtin' like hell. You?"

"Other than being smothered, I'm all right, but..." Tentatively, she reached upward with her foot and discovered a large flat slab had fallen diagonally across them and created an area free of debris, forming an air pocket of sorts. They lay facing each other, but with Sam off to the side a bit.

"Posse's up on top of the ridge. They'll be along."

She nodded, deciding to save her air for more important things like breathing. He cleared his throat. "I meant what I said...before."

"I love you too, Sam. Never stopped." How wonderful it was to finally share her feelings. Now that it was too late.

"Why'n the hell did you run off? Better tell me now. Maybe the last chance you have."

"Oh, Sam... I've always regretted what I did and the way I did it."

"Sorry don't mean shit. I want the truth—all of it. I don't care how bad it is. Was there another man?"

"No. At least, not the way you mean." She struggled to find the words, the words that would make him understand her headlong rush to run away. "I was being blackmailed. It took most of your savings to pay him off. I kept the rest for a new start."

"What'd he have on you? What had you done?"

"Nothing, not really. I just didn't want people—anyone—you—to know I grew up in a New Orleans brothel."

"So you were a whore? *That's* what you were hiding from me?"

"No! I wasn't a whore. But I knew that was what everyone would think, you included. My mother was the madam. She kept me at school and away from the business most of the time, but I was home during the summer. That's when I saw one of the girls have her baby. That's how I knew what to do with Star."

"I wondered about that."

"Sam, I couldn't have people think your wife was a common whore. That's what Thibodaux, who was one of my mother's best customers, was going to tell folks unless I became his mistress. It would've ruined you as a lawman."

"Like you running off didn't. I had to leave the Rangers. I was lucky to get this job as a deputy marshal."

"Oh honey, I'm sorry. I missed you so much, but I had to run. Even though I knew you'd hunt me down."

"I quit looking after they said you died. That fire—did you set it?"

"No! How could you ask such a thing? To my discredit, though, I took advantage of it. I knew if you thought I was dead, you'd quit looking. Anyway, I've set aside almost enough money to pay you back."

"It wasn't the damn money-well, maybe it was a little. You can't imagine how your disappearance hit me. At first, I thought someone had taken you—some outlaw I'd put behind bars. Then I discovered you'd emptied my bank account. I would've strangled you on the spot if I could've gotten ahold of you right then."

"Really?"

"Yeah! But, honey, you took so much more. Dreams for a family-the future I thought we'd have—suddenly it was all gone."

"I'm so sorry," she said, her throat catching. "I shared those same dreams."

Once the posse made it down to the valley floor, Cord sent two men to chase after O'Reilly. "Rest of you, we've got to dig 'em out." With determination, he gazed at the cave opening filled with rock.

"Don't even know if they're alive," said one posse member, Grigsby, a rancher, apparently ready to turn his horse and head home.

"We've gotta try," Cord pleaded. "Miss Nelson saved my wife's life when there was no one else to deliver our son. And Sam Dunaway is a US deputy marshal. As a fellow lawman, I can't give up on him. I hope you won't either."

"Ain't no way they coulda lived through that cave-in. My ranch needs tendin' to." Gathering the reins, Grigsby swung his horse around.

"No! You've been deputized as a member of this posse, and you're not leaving until I say so. I say we form a chain and start diggin'."

The reluctant rancher muttered low, and Cord couldn't quite hear the words. No need. He could pretty much figure out the man's feelings. As long as he obeyed orders, the man could grumble all he wanted.

"Could take days," Luis said. "We'll need reinforcements if they're not close to the opening."

"We'll see how it goes. Unless they found an air pocket, they'll run out of air soon."

"If they survived the initial explosion."

"Yeah." Cord dismounted, then swept his hat off and mopped his forehead with his neckerchief. "Time's a-wasting."

"Hell of a situation." Sam could only move his shoulders a couple of inches either way. His legs were held fast by a heavy boulder. Yet Celine's soft breasts pressed against his chest, causing his cock to ache for release. Hell of a time to get a hard-on.

Celine let out a snort. "Leave it to you to get aroused when we're within minutes of death."

"Glad you find it amusing."

"I'm not *amused*. I'm scared half to death we're going to die, but having your Johnson poking my belly surely gives me some fond memories."

"Nice to know, but we probably shouldn't try to talk so damned much."

He felt her head nod into his shoulder. He shifted, trying to give her more breathing space. "We have a slight chance," he said. "We're pretty close to the mouth of the cave."

In response, her lower body rubbed against his cock. "Stop it," he said. "This ain't the time nor place."

"I can't help it. I need some room. I'm going to smother."

"At this point, I'd smack some sense into you if l could move. As it is, we need to make some noise so they'll know we're alive."

He tried to reach for his gun, but his hand was pinned. Damn. "Can you get the gun from my holster?"

"You're going to fire it? You think that's wise?"

"Hell, no. I'm gonna use it to bang on this dad-blamed stone coffin-just to let 'em know we're still breathing."

"You really think they can hear us through all this rock?"

"Countin' on it."

"But what if they can't?"

"Then we'll die here—with you right where you belong...in my arms."

Sam eased the gun from Celine's hand. "Careful. Don't shoot me." He took the revolver by the butt and managed to open the cylinder and dump the bullets into his other palm. "Hold on to these." He closed the Colt, gripped it by the barrel and struck the large boulder pinning them inside.

Over and over he repeated the blows. He winced, as the sounds were deafening. Hell, deafness was better than suffocating any old day.

Cord and the remaining posse formed a line to dig out the mouth of the cave. At first the loose debris was cleared away quickly. After about an hour's work, they ran into the large boulders sealing the cave shut.

"We're not prepared for this kind of job," Cord said, shaking his head in disgust. He instructed the reluctant rancher to return to town. "We need every able-bodied man and boy. Tell 'em to bring picks, shovels—anything we can dig with."

The rancher shook his head. "Don't know as this is anythin' but a wild-goose chase. Those folks are dead. It's too bad. Miss Nelson just made my wife a new dress, but that's life."

"Just do as you're told. If you don't want to come back...suit yourself. But I'm not giving up on these two. Now go on and git!"

Fists clenched at his sides, the rancher swelled up as if he wanted to fight but then thought better of it. He mounted his horse and headed up the trail to the ridge.

"Hold on." At the head of the line, Luis held up a hand for quiet. "I think I hear something." He leaned against the rock. "Feel it too. There's a vibration that wasn't there before. They're alive."

Cord let out a chuckle. "Damned if you don't have the eyes and ears of a redskin. If we didn't have the same ma and pa, I'd swear you're part Comanche." Cord shook his head, then yelled after the departing rancher, "Hear that, Grigsby? They're alive!"

Celine tried to take a deep breath, but breathing was becoming more and more difficult. Even though she could hear faint sounds of the posse's rescue efforts, she doubted rescue would come in time. "Sam..."

"Save your breath."

"I have to say this. I love you. I've always loved you."

"Hell, Celine. You're giving up. I'm not." He banged the gun butt against the wall of their stifling cave.

"At least we're not alone."

"Now you're just plain maudlin."

Maudlin she might be, but she had to try. "Sam..." She dragged in another breath. "Will you forgive me for what I did? I need to hear you say it...just once."

"I'll say it when we're freed. Not until."

"But..." She needed to know he'd forgiven her, but he wasn't going to give her that little bit of comfort, was he? "How long do you think it's been?"

"Dunno."

She moved about as best she could. If only she could get comfortable and sleep. Then when she woke, they'd either be rescued or dead, in which case, she wouldn't wake up at all. At that gloomy thought, a tremor shuddered its way through her body.

"Gonna be all right. You'll see."

Somehow Sam's words lacked the same ring of conviction they'd had a little while ago. He struck his gun against the stone slab over their heads. Even the vigor of his blow seemed diminished. Truly, they were going to die in this hell-hole of a limestone prison.

Damn O'Reilly and his dynamite! Just when she had a glimmer of hope that she'd have another chance at a life with Sam. Whether he truly forgave her or not, she was still his wife.

In the utter blackness of the cave, Sam touched her cheek gently. "Wish I could see your face," he said a little breathlessly.

"Glad you can't. I probably look a sight all covered in dust." She gave a little cough. If she had to die now, and it was looking very likely at the moment, then at least she was with her husband.

She settled once more in the only moderately comfortable position, her head resting on his shoulder. "Am I too heavy?" she asked.

"Arm's gone way past numb. You're fine."

"Sorry." Because she could hear a vein of amusement in his tone, a smile tugged at her mouth as she drifted, remembering better times.

That day they'd met, years ago, he'd been so handsome, riding up with his guns blazing.

The stagecoach she'd taken to come west had just been robbed by some of the Tyler gang, as it turned out. Rescue came in the form of one tall Texas Ranger. After Sam chased away one of the road agents and captured the second, he escorted the stage safely to the nearest town. She'd been attracted to his rugged good looks immediately, and he to hers. After a whirlwind courtship, they'd married. That first year of marriage, she relished the everyday normality of their life together. Cooking Sam's meals. Planning a family. And making love had been a revelation. Her married life was completely different from the life she'd known in the bordello where she'd grown up, but his duties with the Rangers had taken him away so often. And sometimes for so long.

His absence had left her vulnerable to Thibodaux's threats.

Chapter Fourteen

After what seemed like hours later, Sam willed himself not to give up hope. Celine had fallen asleep—still breathing, though. He forced himself to take shallow breaths. Air almost gone. Thinking fuzzy.

Then a lick of cool air drifted across his ear. Could it be? Had he drifted off? He gave the slab above his head two sharp raps. "We're here!"

A slender shaft of life-giving light...and more air.

"Celine?' He nudged her with his free hand, waiting—no, praying—for a response. Nothing.

"Hurry!"

Over the sounds of rock and stone being dug away, he heard an excited shout. "They're alive."

Now that rescue was at hand, she had to be all right. He patted then smacked her cheek. "Celine, dammit! Wake up."

No response. None that he could see, anyway, despite the slowly widening shaft of daylight. He sucked in his first deep breath of sweet, fresh air.

He shook Celine's shoulder, none too gently either. "Dammit, woman, breathe!"

A memory came to his mind's eye: once he'd seen a squaw revive a newborn baby by breathing into its tiny mouth. Taking another lungful of air, he pressed his lips against Celine's and blew into her mouth. The lush softness of her lips distracted him from his mission, but only for a second or so. No time for his stiffening prick.

"Celine." He murmured her name, then repeated the breath. Barely, just barely, against his chest, he felt the faint flutter of her heart beating.

"Breathe, darlin'. Breathe." He pressed his mouth to hers for another breath. She coughed. Choked, then sputtered, finally drawing in a ragged gasp.

Their rescuers were taking too damn long. "Here! We're over here." Sam felt the boulder at his back being lifted away. He took a deep, deep breath, wincing from the pain. Damn, felt like he'd broken a rib for sure. The aperture widened, and he found himself staring at the sheriff's smiling face.

"You sure are a sight for sore eyes," Sam told Cord with a nod.

"Wish I could say the same. You like some kind of desert creature—one of those nomads," the sheriff said.

"Get Celine out first. She needs some air. Besides, she's laid on my arm until it's useless." With a quick nod, the sheriff reached forward, leaned in, and pulled Celine free from the air pocket.

Relieved, Sam watched as the sheriff picked up her and carried her to freedom.

Once the pressure of her weight was gone, his arm and hand began to tingle, then burn like Hades as the feeling returned.

The sheriff's brother appeared. "Now, let's get you outta here. I've seen enough of this cave to last a lifetime."

"Me too. Careful. My ankle's caught. Don't think it's

broken, though."

Luis and another member of the posse managed to dislodge the stone trapping Sam's ankle, then pulled him free. With an arm around each of their shoulders, they supported him as he staggered from the cave.

Sam started when he emerged. The sun had already to set behind the nearest ridge, and every man in the county seemed to be there. "I see you had some help." He nodded to the sheriff.

"Seemed like the situation called for it," the sheriff said. "Lotta men had come to town for the trial."

Sam held up a hand. "I want to say thanks to everyone. You got us just in time. Don't figure we'd have made it much longer." He looked over to Celine, who sat on a rock, still coated with dust, gulping water from a canteen. His heart sped up at the sight of her alive and well.

One of the men shoved a canteen into Sam's hand. He drank it dry. "I was a bit parched," he said, handing it back to the man who'd given it to him.

"Can you ride?" the sheriff asked.

Sam took a few tentative steps on his sore ankle, then slapped the dust from his clothes. "I can ride...slow," he added with a rueful smile. He limped over to Celine. "You ready?" He held out his hand.

She nodded, then stood and put her arms around his neck. He gazed into her silver—gray eyes and saw acceptance and then the familiar flare of passion. He dipped his lips to hers and tasted their dusty sweetness.

The men who'd gathered around whooped and broke into applause. Celine ducked her head into his chest, her cheeks flaming.

"I've never been so glad to see anyone in my life," she

said. "Are you really all right?"

"I am."

"They said O'Reilly got away. The sheriff sent two men after him but kept everyone else here to help dig us out." As if suddenly self-conscious of her appearance, she pulled back and shook more dust from her hair. "I must look a fright."

Sam brushed the dust from his head. "More like an angel."

The sheriff clapped Sam on the shoulder. "Sorry to break this up. We've still got a killer on the loose. What do you want to do, Marshal? Doubt you're up to riding with the posse."

More than anything, Sam wanted to see O'Reilly pay for what he'd done. "Rather not slow you down. I'll see Celine gets back to your spread. If you don't have him in hand by tomorrow morning, I'll head into town. Need to see if the judge has arrived yet. If not, I'll spell your deputies at the jail."

Cord settled his Stetson on his head. "Sounds like a plan. Let's ride."

Within a few minutes, the sheriff and his posse had mounted and ridden from the valley floor. Dusk had deepened the sky, painting the distant pink granite hills a smoky shade of purple. "You ready?" He nodded at Celine.

"You'll never know how ready." The expression in her silver eyes warmed, giving him a hint of her meaning.

He helped her mount his gelding, then, tamping down a groan, he maneuvered himself up and behind the saddle. He wrapped his arms around her waist, taking the reins in hand. Mindful of his sore ribs, he urged the gelding to a gentle pace. "You sure you're all right?"

She glanced over her shoulder to meet his gaze. "I've been better."

"What are we going to do?" he asked, keeping his tone low.

"After we stop at the sheriff's ranch and I see that Star is all right, I'm going home where I can take a bath and fall into bed. I'm covered in grit and grime. Honestly, I don't know if I'll ever feel clean again."

"And beyond that?"

"What do you mean?" She glanced up at him again. "After the trial, are you coming home with me?"

He felt her back stiffen, her elbows rigid to her sides. "How can I? I've made my life in Kenton Valley, and in case you've forgotten, I've a business to run."

"Your business—that means more to you than sharing a life with me? Having a family?"

"I'm amazed you still want me." He could hear the wonderment in her tone. "I never expected, didn't dare to hope, that you'd take me back."

"Never stopped loving you." He let the words fall softly to her ear. "That's not to say I wasn't ready to bite the heads off rattlers when you left. Even had visions of seeing you behind bars."

"Prison?" Twisting around, she nailed him with a sideways glance. "Really?"

"Damn straight." So much for what he'd thought when he'd first glimpsed her in the store window. Once again, he'd fallen for her bewitching ways.

"What changed your mind?" she asked in a whisper.

"Reckon holding you in my arms and nearly dying might've had something to do with it. I still want a family. Do you?"

"Now that you mention it... Seeing Star with her baby made me ache to hold one of my own, but—"

"But what?"

"You'll still be gone all the time. Now, I understand being a lawman is part of your life. It's who you are. I wouldn't want to change that."

"Well, I sure can't see myself running a dry goods store."

"No, you'd be terrible at it," she said with a smile in her tone.

"Then we're at an impasse." The easy motion of his gelding had lulled him into thinking they might have another chance at love.

"It's too soon to make any rash decisions. We've been through a lot. Let's sleep on it."

"Yeah," he said, chuckling. "Sleep on it." If he had his way, they'd do a lot more than *sleep* on it. He'd come too far to give up now.

It was full-on night by the time they reached the sheriff's Double Star ranch. "I think I've taken root and attached myself to that saddle." Celine hiked her leg over the pommel and slid down from the gelding.

The gelding shied and sidestepped at her sudden movement. Sam winced with pain. "Careful. You spooked him."

"Sorry. I just had to get off. Do you need my help? Your rib must be killing you."

"Only when I breathe...or move," he admitted, then added, "I can manage."

"Who goes there?" One of the sentries the sheriff had

left behind stepped forward, a rifle positioned at his shoulder.

"Marshal Dunaway and Miss Nelson," Sam said. "O'Reilly got away. Any sign he might've doubled back?"

The cowboy shook his head. "All's quiet."

After Sam dismounted, he turned to Celine. "My horse needs a good feed." He turned and pulled her into his arms. "I sort of had another idea about how to spend to night."

"I figured you did, but I'd say that's less than likely. Go on. See to your horse." She patted Sam's buttocks and watched him lead the gelding to the stable.

Celine opened the door and found Mrs. Crayton rocking by the fireplace. Her eyes were puffy and red, but there was a plate of biscuits she must have made on the table. "Did they catch that no-good varmint who killed my good man? If they did, I hope they strung him up on the spot."

"Wish I could say they did, but he nearly killed the marshal and me. Sadly, he got away in the process."

The woman nodded toward the table. "I fixed some vittles. Reckoned someone would show up and eat 'em."

Celine's stomach rumbled. "Thank you, Mrs. Crayton. It's been a while since we ate." Betty jumped up. "I'll just heat up that stew."

"No, ma'am. Let me. Why don't you go to bed? You've had a long day. How are Star and the baby?"

"Never saw such a stubborn woman in all my life. I tell you no good will come of her getting up on her feet and taking care of her babe, not barely a day old. Stubborn.

Stubborn," she muttered, shaking her head. "Only thing she'd let me do was cook and wash nappies. Still, 'twas good to have something to do. Guess I would've gone crazy otherwise." She burst into a bout of sobbing. "He was a good man. They had no call to kill him."

Celine pulled Betty into her arms. "Now then. You go ahead and cry."

Her tears subsided in a bit. Then she took a good look at Celine. "Heavens, you're covered in dirt. What in tarnation happened to ya?"

Without going into too much detail, Celine told her about being buried in the cave-in.

"Both of you? It's a miracle they got you out. Let's get you out of those clothes."

"I have a change of clothing, and I'm sure the sheriff has something the marshal can wear."

"So you and the marshal was penned in there together. My, my."

"It's all right. We're married. It's just we've been separated for a great while."

"I see." The grieving widow nodded knowingly.

Celine set the pot of stew on the cookstove to warm, then ran upstairs to see Star. Tapping on the door, she said, "It's only me."

"Come in. Come in. I can't believe you're back. What about the Irishman? Did they catch him?" Star smiled down at her nursing baby.

At sight of the blissful expression on her friend's face, Celine's heart clenched. Would she ever have a child of her own? Could she and Sam ever come to an agreement? "No, but I doubt he'll show his face around here again."

Star straightened her shoulders. "I'd lynch him myself

if I could catch him."

"That makes two of us."

After giving Celine an up-and-down glance, Star sighed. "I'd let you hold the baby, but you look a trifle worn from your ordeal."

Celine looked down at her filthy dress and let out a bark of laughter. "You have no idea. I'll tell you later, but may Sam and I spend the night? He thinks he might have a broken rib."

"Of course you may. What happened?"

"I'll tell you after I get out of these clothes and get some food in Sam's belly."

"The Irishman, he didn't...?"

Celine stopped at the doorway and shook her head. "No, but it was close."

Celine slid into the deep copper tub of steaming, soapy water with a sigh. Even though she'd washed her hands and face before sitting down to a hearty dinner of beef stew and biscuits slathered with creamy butter, she doubted she'd ever get really clean. Honestly, dirt and grit from the cave-in had worked its way into every crevice and cranny of her body. Lugging pails of hot water up to the second floor had been a backbreaking chore, especially after so much time on horseback, but it was worth the effort. The heavenly heat of the water seeped into her muscles and relaxed the tension. The fragrant French-milled lavender soap teased her nose and made her feel like a real woman again.

After supper, Sam had gone out to the bunkhouse, muttering something about cleaning up. Somehow she doubted his bunkhouse ablutions would be as enjoyable as hers.

Her face was red and tender from all the sun, but, using a large sponge, she soaped and scrubbed every other inch of her body. Then she pulled the pins from her hair, shook her head and let the tangled mass fall onto her shoulders. Sliding farther down in the tub, she dipped her head back to wet her hair. Coming up for air, she scrubbed her tresses vigorously, dipped and rinsed it again. Finally, she stood and was about to wrap a bath sheet around her body when the bedroom door opened.

"Don't let me stop you." Sam's low drawl sent an army of goose bumps to her arms. He stood in the doorway, tall and handsome as always, even though the britches he wore were a size too large.

"You ever heard of knocking?" she said, shivering under his heated gaze.

"And miss seeing you in the altogether? What would be the fun in that?" He eased his arms around her waist, pulling her to his chest. "You smell a damn sight better than you did in the cave."

She snorted. "Well, so do you." She tucked in the loose edge of the bath sheet. "How's your rib?"

"Don't reckon it's broken after all. Bruised and sore as the dickens, though."

"Does that mean I need to be careful with you?"

"Not too careful, I hope."

She smiled, her heart soaring to be back in his arms again. Who knew it would merely take being buried alive to get her there? "Help me with my hair."

"I'm no lady's maid," he said with a half-smile. "Tell me what to do."

She picked up the extra towel Star had so thoughtfully provided and wrapped it around her head. "Dry it. Then you need to brush out the tangles."

Together they dried her hair with the towel, then she sat as he began to pull the brush through her long tresses.

"I used to do this for you every night."

"Every night when you were at home...anyway."

"Now..." Gently, he rapped the top of her head with the back of the brush.

"Ow! And don't pull. Brush it in sections, then I want a single braid down the back." "Bossy, aren't you?" he said with a smile in his voice. "You have the most beautiful hair of any woman I've ever known. Don't know why you wear it in that bun thing."

"It was part of my new self. Selma Nelson is plain with no fripperies—except on the dresses she makes."

"Right."

Eventually, he brushed out all the tangles. The long smooth strokes lulled her into a sense of easy comfort. "I always loved it when you brushed my hair, Sam. I really missed your touch."

"That all you missed?"

She allowed a smile. "I missed your body heat in the winter. And I missed the way you made love to me." She gave a little huff. "What I did not miss was your never being around."

"That's not likely to change in the future."

"I know." She rose from the chair and twined her arms around his neck. "Oh, Sam..." He cupped her bottom and kissed her. She opened to him, his tongue battling with hers. He picked her up and carried her to the bed, then gently laid her down.

"You're wearing too many clothes, Marshal," she teased from the soft feather bed.

"Easily remedied, Mrs. Dunaway." He unbuttoned his shirt, then unbuckled his belt.

"It has been a very long time since anyone called me that," she murmured, knowing and dreading the inevitable decision to be made. But not now. Now was about something just as inevitable-warmth and passion. Being close again to the man she would always love.

Sam let the borrowed denim trousers fall to the floor with a chuckle. "The sheriff is a bigger man."

He stood lean-hipped, his muscled thighs quivering. His cock jutted thick from the black patch that arrowed up his belly.

"Not from my vantage point," she murmured. If the sheriff's prick was bigger than Sam's, her friend was a very lucky woman indeed.

Sam sat on the side of the bed, tugging off his boots while she waited. She'd missed his loving so many nights after running away. Pleasuring herself was a poor substitute for the passion they'd found in their marriage bed.

Then, before she could have imagined it, he was lying beside her, their bodies skin to skin. "I missed you so."

He stopped her words with his fingers across her lips. He left a trail of kisses on her neck and shoulders, down to her breasts.

"And I missed these," he said.

"They are attached to *me*," she protested.

"Missed you too-when I allowed myself. Otherwise, I was highly pissed off."

"You might've mentioned that once or twice."

He took a nipple in his mouth and sucked hard. A spike of desire shot to her core, her body bucking. Then he left another trail of kisses down her belly. He parted her folds, sliding one finger into her wet heat. She moaned, her hips moving from side to side. "You like torturing me, don't you?"

"Don't you think you deserve it?"

"Maybe a little."

Getting to his knees, he parted her thighs, leaving more kisses until she thought she might die. His cock was heavy against her thigh. He slipped a second finger inside her cleft. "It's been a while," she warned.

"Better have." He stretched her gently, then removed his fingers, licking them. "You still taste like honey."

"You're crazy if you think that." "Crazy about you."

"Love me, Sam. Love me like you used to."

Needing no additional encouragement, Sam thrust home, burying his cock to the hilt in her wet heat. Slowly, he began to move. With each stroke, her body adjusted to his size until he felt as if he'd never been away.

Home. He was home with the woman he'd always loved. The woman he thought had betrayed him and he'd had lost forever.

Her body rose to meet his with each sure stroke until they came together in a burst of blinding heat. His body shuddering with the strength of his climax, he gasped her name and she cried his.

Spent, he fell to the side to keep from crushing her. "I thought I remembered what it was like. I'd forgotten how it was after all. I really needed reminding." Yes, his wife was worth fighting for. He wouldn't give up until she agreed to come back to Austin with him.

"Sam?" Her slender fingers caressed his cheek. "You shaved," she commented, not getting right to the point.

What now? he wondered, cocking an eyebrow. "Yeah?"

"Do you think we can make it this time around?"

Oh, her tone was sweet, but his wife definitely had something on her mind. "I do. But this time, some things will have to change." He had to make it clear he wasn't going to be a pushover just because they'd made love.

"And they will. Now I have something to occupy my time when you're away. I have the shop. I'm even thinking about leaving the boardinghouse and converting the attic space into a bedroom and sitting room. There would even be enough room for a nursery."

"Are you saying you want children? My children?"

"Of course I do." Rolling toward him, she gazed at him so sincerely he almost forgot to breathe.

"But life got complicated when Antoine Thibodaux Louisiana, showed up. He'd known my father and all about my mother and me. You weren't home, and it was just easier to run away. Until you rode into town the other day, I'd given up all hope of ever having a family or your children. But seeing Star and Cord with their sweet baby reminded me that having your baby was what I'd always wanted."

"Oh, my darlin' Celine." He levered onto one elbow, then sat up. Gathering her hands in his, he said softly, "I want you to move to Austin with me."

Her honey-brown brows drew together, and her body grew less pliant. Less willing. Less his.

"We don't have to decide this tonight. Don't spoil things. Not yet."

"We'll have to decide soon." His breath caught in his throat. After being with her again, he wouldn't—no, couldn't-give her up. One of them would have to compromise. And to his way of thinking, since she was the one who'd upped and run, she'd be the one to concede.

"But not tonight. Please not tonight."

"All right, but *soon*." He gave her ass a love tap. Fair warning, he wouldn't just roll over and do whatever the hell she wanted.

Chapter Fifteen

"Sam. Sam, wake up."

"Uh," he grunted. "What?" He raised his head and pried his eyes open. For the briefest of moments, the sight of Celine lying beside him startled him. But just as quickly, the memory of their loving flooded his mind and senses. He moved closer, seeking her warmth, ready to take advantage of her sweetness once more.

She shoved his hands away from her lush breasts. "Sam! Stop it! I heard something. Someone's in the house."

"It's probably Mrs. Crayton doing something for the baby, or maybe the sheriff and the posse are back." He lay back on the pillow and shut his eyes. Entirely too early to stay awake if she wasn't...

"No! Mrs. Crayton is sleeping on a cot in the room with Star and the baby. Sounds like someone who's trying to be quiet. It's not your normal moving-around sounds."

"I don't hear anything. Go back to sleep." He rolled over, determined to go back to sleep.

She poked his shoulder. "Hush and listen."

Thump.

"There is it again. You have to do something."

Right. Sounded like someone bumped into a chair. "Yeah, I heard it." He sat up, swung his legs over the side of the bed and stood. He grabbed the borrowed denims from the chair beside the bed and drew them on, buttoned the fly and cinched the belt tightly around his waist since the sheriff's trousers had a tendency to slide down his hips. Picking up his gun belt and Colt, he drew the six-shooter from the holster and padded softly to the bedroom door.

"Stay here," he cautioned. Dang woman was already half-dressed and looked like she was of a mind to follow.

"But—"

"Stay," he hissed. After opening the door, he eased into the hallway. From the sounds below, someone had bumped into a piece of furniture more than once, followed by a stream of low curses.

Sam walked to the top of the stairs, eased one foot down, then another. Third step creaked. Six-shooter held low at his side, he froze.

Listened.

Not a sound.

Shooting his host would be a definite black mark, not to mention inconvenient and difficult to justify. "Sheriff Taylor, if that's you, you'd best call out. I'm armed and ready."

Then he heard a rush of footsteps toward the front of the house. He flew the rest of the way downstairs and caught up with the intruder at the already open door. Sam tackled the man, and they tumbled through the screened door.

The intruder sprang to his feet, moving warily to the far end of the porch. "How in bleedin' hell did ye get out of that shite cave?"

"O'Reilly!" Sam scrambled to his feet and rushed the outlaw, swinging his fist into the Irishman's gut. "Going to sneak into the house with two lone women and a baby? Going to play your dirty games with them, were you?"

The Irishman kicked Sam in the ribs. He gasped with pain and jumped back to catch his breath. "You no-account mick. You did your damnedest to kill us, but we were tougher than you figured." He punctuated each word with a blow to the intruder's chin, his gut, his nose. Sam smiled as he felt and heard the man's nose break.

Grabbing his face, O'Reilly staggered and then hit the dirt. "Gah!" He sprang to his feet, spat blood and pulled a long blade from his belt. "I'll cut your bleedin' heart out this time." Crouching low, he lunged.

Sam jumped to the side, averting the blade. The Irishman drew back, but before he could throw the knife, Sam flew at the Irishman again. They tumbled off the porch and onto the dusty ground with a thud. They came to a puddle of blood darkening the earth. Out of one eye, Sam saw that the sentry's throat had been slit. More of the Irishman's handiwork. Given there was no sign of the other sentry. Likely he'd met the same fate.

"I'd be doing the world a favor if I strung you up here and now." Sam sat astride the Irishman with his hands around the killer's throat. "You're a sneak and a coward. You prey on women and children who're too weak to fight back. Low-down, lily-livered bastard."

O'Reilly kicked and struggled, clawing at Sam's fingers. Reluctantly, Sam released his death grip, settling instead for slugging the Irishman with the butt of his Colt.

"You'll need this."

Sam looked up to see Celine standing in the doorway, a blanket wrapped around her upper body, holding a rope.

"Where'd you find that?"

"In the stable. Where else?"

"Dressed like that?"

Grasping the blanket tightly, she growled, "Do you want the rope or not?"

Holding his ribs, he struggled to his feet. He closed the distance between them and took the coiled rope." Smart. What if I hadn't won? O'Reilly would have you stripped and begging for your life by now."

"I knew you'd prevail," she said with a sweet smile. "He's no match for a real man."

"See any sign of the other guard?" He knelt beside O'Reilly and began binding his hands.

Her expression grew somber. "Yes. He's dead, just like this one." She rubbed her upper arms and shivered.

"You're cold." He shot her a concerned look. "Best get inside. I'll take care of this varmint."

She nodded and left him to finish his task.

Once back in her bedroom, Celine was tempted to return to their bed but she was too keyed up to rest. Then came the thundering sound of horses' hooves. The posse. Instead falling into the bed where she and Sam had just made love, she rallied, pulled on the top of her shirtwaist and ran downstairs to the kitchen. After a long day and night on horseback, the men were bound to be tired and hungry. She started a fire in the cookstove and rechecked the icebox to see what she could feed a gang of hungry men.

She heard one man running for the stairs. She poked her head around the door to the kitchen and spied the sheriff. "They're all right," she called. "O'Reilly never got that far."

The sheriff's broad shoulders relaxed as he turned and sat on one of the steps, exhaustion clearly written across his face and body. His elbows on his knees, he shut his eyes and rested his head in his hands.

"I'm heating up the stove. I'll have y'all something to eat pretty soon."

He looked up, meeting her gaze. "You shouldn't be on your feet. Not after what you've been through."

"I'm fine. Don't know when I've felt better," she said, unable to hide the lilt in her voice. "After what you all did for Sam and me, I owe you a hot meal, at the very least."

"Much appreciated, ma'am." He stood and headed up the stairs to see his wife and new baby son.

By the time the rest of the posse had seen their mounts fed and watered, Celine had a large pot of coffee perking, fresh biscuits baking, and bacon frying in the heavy iron skillet. The aroma of fresh coffee and sizzling bacon set her stomach to growling.

After caring for their mounts, most of the posse had split off, opting to return to their homes. For the sheriff, his brother Luis and two remaining members of the posse, Celine whipped up a large bowl of milk gravy to go along with the biscuits. She set the crockery bowl of gravy on the table beside two big platters of bacon and hot biscuits. "Dig in! That should keep starvation from the door until you make it back home."

There were "Thank you, ma'ams" all around.

Standing beside Sam, Celine smiled. "Happy to oblige. And I'm the one who should be thanking you. The marshal and I wouldn't be here without your help." Sam gazed up at her with—dare she think it-love glowing in his whiskey-brown eyes.

Unable to keep from yawning, she felt the blood rush to her cheeks again.

A mischievous twinkle lit Sam's eyes as he looked up at her. Reaching behind her, he patted her butt and then grabbed a couple of biscuits and several strips of bacon for himself.

"I'll leave you men to it, then." Still blushing, she ran upstairs, but not before she heard the men's guffaws.

She eased open the bedroom door where Star and the baby were sleeping. All was right with their world.

"Selma?" Star pushed up on her elbows.

"Sorry. I didn't mean to wake you. And I guess you might as well start calling me Celine. I've started thinking of myself that way again."

Star raised an eyebrow. "You and the marshal?"

Celine nodded. "I'll tell you more tomorrow. Go back to sleep." She eased the door shut. But what would she tell Star? Nothing was really settled except Sam wasn't going to arrest her *and* he still loved her. But would they have a life together or not? That was the real question.

After chowing down the quick breakfast, Sam trudged up the stairs. Surely Celine had gone back to bed and wasn't waiting to argue about their future. Heaven knew she needed the rest. Hell, he wouldn't mind a little himself.

Yet the same questions plagued him. Where would they go from here? He'd be leaving town as soon as the trial was over to go back to Austin for his next assignment.

She'd either go with him or not.

True he spent most of his time either in Austin or moving around the state as his duties as a US marshal called for.

Was it fair for him to expect her to leave her business? He shook his head. To hell with it. Their future wasn't something he wanted to deal with right now. He had too much else on his mind.

As soon as he reached the top of the stairs, Celine emerged from the other bedroom. "Sam?"

Damn. Not ready to entertain more discussion, he said, "I'm heading into town with O'Reilly," he said. "Why don't you go back to bed?"

Giving him a tentative half smile, she glanced at the room where they'd spent the night together. "Don't you think we should talk?"

"Not now."

"Later, then? When?"

He shrugged. What was the point? She didn't want to leave Kenton Valley, and his job was based at the state capital. "I need to get the prisoner to the jail." The Irishman had spent what Sam hoped was an uncomfortable few hours chained in the barn. The sooner the man was behind bars, the better Sam would like it.

"When will you be back? I think we should talk before you go back to Austin. That's where you live now, isn't it?"

"I rent a room in a boardinghouse. I'm not there much, but it's where I hang my hat."

"Like I have at the Foleys'?"

"Yeah, like that." Any other time, he'd head back to Austin once the trial was over. But this occasion was different—yeah, different all right. "Don't suppose you're coming back to town today?"

Celine shook her head. "Mrs. Crayton needs to get her husband buried. I ought to stay with Star for as long as she needs me." She chewed her full bottom lip, then said, "I want to see you again. We really need to have that discussion about our future."

"Don't reckon we have one...unless you're planning on selling out and moving to Austin?"

"There's a lot to think about. It's not something I can decide and accomplish overnight. I've already promised some of young ladies I'd make their dresses for the spring Grange dance."

"A dance, you say? Been a while since..." He shook his head, trying to remember how it felt to be young and excited about a dance at the Grange hall.

"I can't disappoint them. The dance is two weeks away. What with giving Star a hand here and making those dresses, I'll have my hands full."

"Understand that. Two weeks from now? I'll be back in Austin, or I'll be back on the trail-no telling where."

She nodded. "I know. I remember how it was when you were in the Rangers."

"And I remember how it was when I came home and found you missing." He'd tried to keep the edge from his voice but failed.

She averted her gaze. "I thought you'd forgiven me. I guess I was wrong."

He set his hands on her shoulders, wanting to reassure her. "I have. Just can't forget how it felt. Old hurts take time to fade."

She pulled away. "Go to town, Sam."

Her tone was flat, her expression flatter. "I hope I'll see

you before you go." She gathered her skirts and slammed the bedroom door behind her, leaving him standing alone.

Damn woman. What did she want from him?

He stomped downstairs. No matter, he had a job to do. And do it he would.

Celine gazed out the window, watching Sam, the sheriff and what was left of the posse as they loaded five dead men into the Crayton's wagon. A manacled O'Reilly was forced to ride with the bodies. Served him right. So much violence in such a short time, some of which she was responsible for. Yet she couldn't say she regretted the part she'd played in turning two of the outlaws against each other.

Poor brave Mrs. Crayton. Her back was straight as she rode home accompanied by one of the posse. Her husband had died needlessly, as had the two guards.

Celine picked up a tray of food and carried it upstairs. "It's me," she said with a quick rap on the bedroom door. Her friend was already on her feet, leaning over the small cradle. "Sit and have some breakfast," Celine said.

"All right..." Star sat with a huff.

Celine set the tray across her friend's knees. "Before Mrs. Crayton left, she said you were to stay in bed for the next week, preferably two weeks."

"I've already been up and suffered no ill effects. Mrs. Crayton's ideas of childbirth are mired in the Middle Ages. I was mighty glad to have her here, though, but I'm fine now. To my way of thinking, women through the ages have been having babies in the fields and gone back to work."

"No, that was the *dark* ages." Celine set her hands on

her hips. "You've had a baby, and while some women out of necessity might've been forced to go back to work, you aren't. You can take it easy. I'm staying here until you're ready to be up and about."

"I'm ready to be up and about now. But while I drink my coffee, why don't you tell me what happened with you and the marshal."

While Star ate her breakfast, Celine proceeded to regale her about the incidents leading up to the cave-in, including that transformative event, until a loud, angry squall interrupted her.

Star smiled and tugged at the neckline of her gown. "I may be a new mother, but I already know what that cry means."

Celine reached for the baby, then, feeling the damp diaper, she asked, "May I change him? Please."

"Be my guest. If I'm not mistaken, you'll be having some of your own someday soon. Good practice."

While Celine changed the baby boy, she wondered if she ever really would have one of her own. Given the current state of affairs, it wasn't something she could take for granted.

"So, what are you going to do?"

"I really don't want to sell my business. I do so enjoy being a part of the town. And I have three dresses I'm supposed to make for the Grange spring dance. How can I disappoint those girls?"

"And after that? You know, Austin isn't that far. Maybe there's some way you can both have what you want."

"A compromise? I don't know. Sam's not the compromising type."

"Neither, it seems to me, are you."

Chapter Sixteen

Sam slammed the steel-barred door closed. "Reckon that ought to keep you. Since you killed Barnes's partners, I don't expect anyone will be breaking you out."

"Bleedin' peeler. Ye kept me tied up like I was a feckin' barn animal."

"Quit your bellyaching. After what you did, you're lucky I didn't kill you on the spot. But you'll be dancing at the end of a rope soon enough."

From the other cell, Arvil Barnes held his head in his hands. "Booker, Fisher—they's dead?"

"That's a fact," Sam said with a smile. "This mick here was the powder man they hired to effect your escape." He jerked his thumb in the Irishman's direction. "He killed 'em, all right. Even used his store of dynamite trying to kill me. Reckon when the judge arrives, we'll have two trials and two hangings."

Barnes let out with a spate of obscenities, and O'Reilly replied with language equally colorful.

Turning on his heel, Sam left the prisoners to their *discussion*.

Back in the outer office, Sam found the judge had arrived. Judge Harley Riordan was gray-haired, tall and imposing, as one might expect of a man of his position. Sam quickly introduced Cord and his brothers.

"Glad to meet you," the judge responded. "Now, where might I spend the night?" "Boardinghouse down the street. That's where I'm lodged."

The judge nodded his agreement. As they walked over to the boardinghouse, Sam brought him up-to-date regarding the preceding days' events and the need for a second trial.

"You've been busy. And you've reunited with your *late* wife? Am I to understand that correctly?"

"Yes, sir. Now that is an even longer story. For the time being, we are reunited. The final outcome, however, is still uncertain."

"Marriage settles a man. I highly recommend it. It's especially important if you want to advance in law enforcement."

"She has a business here in town, the dry-goods store." Sam jerked his thumb in the store's direction. "She's a dressmaker too."

"Surely she won't keep that up when she moves to Austin."

"That's the part I'm not certain about. She's strong-willed."

"Hmph. You're her husband. She'll have to do as you say."

Sam let out a guffaw. "If it was only that simple."

"Show some spine, man. Give her an ultimatum. She needs to know you mean business." Somewhat against his better judgment and knowing how contrary Celine was, he shook his head. But an ultimatum might just do the trick if she really loved him as much as she said and he gave her no choice.

*

Celine spent a wonderful though busy day tending to Star's baby and Star herself when she would allow it. Still there were the interminable nappies to wash.

Celine held the baby in her lap, marveling at his tiny, perfect features and his just-bathed, clean-baby smell. "Do you know what you'll name him yet?"

"Sam and I discussed it last night for the few minutes we saw each other. It'll be something to honor his ma's forbears."

"With names like Cordero and Luis, I thought there must be some Mexican heritage somewhere."

"Cord's ma was pure Spanish. Her grandfather was a *grandee* from Spain. She died in childbirth when the twins were around five or six. I barely remember her. To my child's eye, she was very beautiful. But my own ma and some of the other women in town treated her like she was trash. That might be another of her reasons she didn't want me to stay here to marry Cord."

"What about Cord's father? What was his name? I'd only heard him referred to as Mr. Tate."

"That would be wonderful. Carl would've loved having the baby named after him."

"You know you could even name the baby Carlos, and maybe use your father's name as his first or middle name."

Star wrinkled her nose. "Well, everyone calls my pa Buck, but his real name is Ezekiel Wilbur Tyler. I wouldn't wish a moniker like that on my precious little one."

"I know-what about Carlos Tyler Tate? Now that's a mouthful for such a wee one, but it's much nicer and blends the two families."

"I love it, but I'll let Cord think he came up with the name with just a little judicious nudging. It's his first son, after all."

Celine chuckled. Devious woman. "Good idea."

Back at the sheriff's office, Sam, Tate and the judge sat around the sheriff's desk. After a brief deliberation, the jury had found Arvil Barnes guilty of murdering the sheriff's wife. With even less time to deliberate, Judge Riordan sentenced him to be hanged.

"That's one trial out of the way," Sam said. He'd especially enjoy seeing justice done so efficiently and properly in this particular case. No one should get away scot-free after killing a woman and unborn babe.

"Now, how many men has this fellow O'Reilly killed?" Riordan asked.

The sheriff spoke up. "After rancher Tom Crayton, he killed Hunt and Fisher, plus the two men I stationed to watch over the women at the ranch while we were out looking for him."

"Five men, three of them innocent bystanders." Riordan shook his head. "At least your first wife and baby have their justice, Sheriff Tate."

"Yeah." Tate nodded.

"Do we need to have five trials?" Sam asked. "My wife saw three of the killings but said it was Fisher who shot Crayton, but O'Reilly finished him off. And we found the bloody knife on O'Reilly that he used to kill the two guards."

"One trial will be enough to hang him," the judge said with a shrug.

The sheriff set his hat on his head. "I'm heading home. Judge, you and the marshal are welcome to have dinner with us."

"No, indeed." Riordan got to his feet. "I wouldn't dream of putting your wife out. The fare at the boardinghouse is plentiful and good."

"I'll pass also," Sam said, standing as well. "Thank you, though. I'll have dinner with the judge." Then as an afterthought, he added, "Tell my wife we'll need her to testify to what she saw, first thing tomorrow morning."

He dug a piece of paper from his pocket. "And if you'll take her this note. I await her decision." That should get her attention. And show her he meant business.

Waiting until he and Riordan were out in the street, Riordan said, "So you're giving her an ultimatum. Good."

"I am. Told her if she didn't come with me, I'd divorce her." "Good man. That'll bring her around."

"You don't know my wife. She's anything but predictable."

Riordan let out a guffaw. "Reckon you're about to find out."

Sam shook his head. "That's what I'm afraid of"

Celine paced from one end of the front porch to the other. Last night over supper, Sheriff Tate had said the second trial would likely end today. That meant the hangings would take place as soon as the gallows was built. There was absolutely no conceivable reason for Sam to continue to ignore her. If the sheriff could come home for his supper, why couldn't Sam come with him?

It was almost time for supper, and the last two nights

she'd cooked enough for an army of lawmen, not to mention one stubborn US marshal.

She heard the horse and rider before she saw them. Standing on tiptoe, she squinted into the sun.

Dammit! One horse and rider, not two.

She folded her arms across her chest as she waited for the sheriff to dismount and tie up his buckskin gelding.

"Well, what's his excuse this time?" The bitter words seemed to spit out of their own accord. "Sorry. I don't mean to take my anger out on you, Sheriff. It's not your fault my husband is determined to drive me to distraction."

The sheriff swept off his Stetson and slapped it against his thigh, sending a cloud of trail dust into the air. "You'll have to come to town tomorrow morning and testify against O'Reilly. You're our only witness to Hunt's and Fisher's deaths."

"Oh—" The very thought of testifying... She'd have to admit she'd incited the killing spree with all her false talk of gold. "I guess I am. I hadn't considered that."

The sheriff dug in his pocket. "Got a note from the marshal. I s'pect you'll want to read it in private." He ducked inside the house. Probably afraid she'd turn emotional when she read it.

Her hands shook as she unfolded the note. Quickly she scanned the words. "Of all the ornery, stubborn..." At that point, words failed.

It's time to make up your mind. Come with me to Austin or stay in the Valley, it's up to you. But if you stay, we're done. I'll see a lawyer about ending this travesty of a marriage.

"I'll show you who's done." She ran inside the house, where Star was setting the table for supper. She looked up, her red brows pulling together in a frown.

"What's wrong now?"

"He sent me a note. A blasted note!" Pacing from one side of the room to the other, Celine waved the offending piece of paper in the air. "It contains an ultimatum. Either I go with him, or he'll divorce me."

Star smiled. "I wouldn't worry. He's just trying to get your attention."

"He could've had my attention every night this week, but he's stayed in town on one pretext or another."

"I'm sure with the judge in town, that..."

"I don't care about that damned judge. Sam's flat-out avoiding me. Trying to weaken my resolve. I'll show him." She clenched her fists at her sides.

"Don't do anything rash, Celine. Give yourself some time to calm down."

"If you'll be all right here tonight, I'll take my buggy into town and face him. I have to go tomorrow for the trial anyway. We might as well settle this tonight."

Chapter Seventeen

As soon as her mare and buggy were ready, Celine wasted no time in striking out for town. The miles flew by, fueled by her anger and the mare's excitement at being let out of the confines of the stable.

Sam Dunaway would soon find he couldn't dictate to her. How dare he give her such a rude ultimatum? She'd never agree to divorce him.

No, *never*.

What was the need anyway? He loved her as much as he ever had. At least that was what he'd said the night they'd made love. And her love for him was certainly as strong as ever. Lying next to him in the cramped space of the air pocket had surely proved that. In spite of those dire circumstances, she'd experienced the same giddiness she'd had the first time they met.

Once she entered town, she drove the buggy straight to the livery behind the boardinghouse.

Mr. Foley emerged, greeting her with his wide, crooked smile as he helped her down from the buggy. "Been a while, Miz Nelson—reckon I oughta say Miz Dunaway."

"Never mind about all that. I'm still the same person, no matter what name you call me by. Your wife still serving supper?"

He glanced over his shoulder at the sun. "Reckon they're winding up 'bout now. Best hurry."

"Great. I'm starving." She picked up her skirt and ran for the back door. Inside, she stopped in the kitchen long enough to inveigle the Foley's cook, Felicity, into making her a quick ham sandwich.

"Now, we still got plenty of food. I'm happy to fix you a plate."

"Thank you, but a sandwich is all I need. Is the marshal around?"

"Him and the judge are in the parlor smoking they's cigars."

"Thanks." Celine picked up the biscuit and ham sandwich, then whipped up to her room on the second floor. A change of clothing and a bit of freshening her appearance was needed before she faced her stubborn husband.

Since coming to Kenton Valley, she'd seldom found the need to wear any of her finery. Time she showed off her dressmaking skills to a more appreciative audience. And tomorrow she would reopen the store and get cracking on those three dresses.

But first, she had to tackle her husband and change his mind about where their future lay.

She donned her favorite dress, a two-piece garment of wine-colored satin, white Chantilly lace collar and cuffs and a cable-rope belt ending with tassels. A gathering of pleats at the hem and on the train skimmed the floor nicely. A lightly padded bustle was her only concession to the overblown Victorian styles. She gazed into the looking glass. Her skin was a little too tan from all the sun to be fashionable. No matter. She pinched her cheeks and delicately applied the tiniest bit of pale color to her lips. She preened from one side to the other, inspecting her stylish appearance. Garnet-and-gold earrings dangled and flashed at her ears. Just let him see what he'd be missing.

Just then, a nagging doubt overcame her usual sense of self-confidence. Surely, she should just be grateful he wasn't going to arrest her for stealing all his savings. Even if she couldn't bend him to her way of thinking, she would still pay back the monies she'd taken.

Stop it. Time they came to a decision that would be palatable to both. Yes, they would.

She slipped on the cordovan, kid leather pumps, then selected a carved ivory stick fan, opened it and cooled her warm cheeks before sliding it into a beaded reticule.

Enough.

Time to face her husband.

Sam leaned back in the comfortable high-backed chair, a Cuban cigar in one hand and a snifter of the judge's fine brandy in the other. "I could get used to this, Judge."

"You're not likely to find such on the trail, Dunaway."

"Don't I know it. He took another puff on the cigar. "I have to say, I admire the way the legal process works, and the authority with which you assumed control over the court intrigues me. Hell, I even enjoyed the showmanship the defense attorney demonstrated."

"That's why you need your wife at your side to make a suitable home for you. With the proper education and tutelage, I foresee a future for you in state politics, son. First thing I recommend you do is to read law. The University of Texas has a mighty fine law school. I like you, and I'm prepared to take you under my wing." He puffed on his cigar, then nodded. "See to it that you advance."

"I don't know about." Sam shook his head even as he savored the brandy's rich taste. "I'll be the first to admit I find the judicial process very interesting, but I must confess I enjoy being on the trail, seeing that justice is done."

"You won't be young forever, and you'll still see that justice is done. Seize the opportunity when it's presented. If you wait," Riordan paused, "the opportunity might not come again." Sam nodded. Studying law with Riordan as a mentor would certainly mean a big change in his future. Someday he would be able to afford a nice house and provide well for any children he and Celine might have.

"Gentlemen..."

The dulcet tones of a woman—and not just any woman either—interrupted Sam's train of thought. He sat forward. "Celine?" His mind whirled at the sight of her. Keeping his gaze off her lustrous skin, her shining hair arranged in honeyed curls instead of a tight old-maid's knot proved near impossible. Her tiny waist—jeez, he could span it with his hands. What was she up to? Surely her presence meant she'd decided to leave with him.

Together, Sam and the judge put out their cigars and stood, although how Sam managed to stand without his knees knocking was beyond him. "Celine, this is Judge Harvey Riordan. Judge Riordan, my wife, Celine."

The judge nodded his approval, then bent over her outstretched hand. "Very pleased to make your acquaintance, my dear."

Celine seated herself on a settee across from the two men, giving them a winning smile. What in blue blazes was she up to?

"I wasn't expecting you until tomorrow," Sam said, his tone gruffer than he intended. An uneasy feeling gathered in his gut. Her sweet mood was unsettling, to say the least. She was definitely up to something.

"I thought I'd better come back to town this evening rather than return tomorrow morning."

"Mrs. Tate is doing all right?" Sam asked, sitting down.

"Indeed. I don't think I've ever seen anyone recover so fast from giving birth."

The judge harrumphed. "Please give her my regards the next time you encounter her." "Most assuredly, I shall, Your Honor." She smiled sweetly, showing a dimple in one cheek.

The judge gave a polite bow. "If you'll excuse me, I believe I'll retire to my room. I have some case law to review."

"Very nice meeting you, Your Honor."

"Likewise. I trust we'll be seeing you in the state capital soon."

Sam waited until Riordan had vacated the sitting room. "What the hell are you up to now?"

"I've come to talk to my husband about the rather rude note I received."

"Wasn't rude. Just plain speech."

She leaned forward, settling her slender fingers lightly on his knee. His leg gave an involuntary jump and his trousers grew tight.

"You're all dressed up tonight," she said. "If I didn't

know better, I'd say you were gambler who plied his trade on a steamboat."

"No such thing." He stood, then paced over to the window, gazing out on the street. "Enough of this foolishness, Celine. Are you coming with me or not?" He turned to face her, hoping his expression unreadable. So much depended on her response.

"I came to see why you couldn't settle here in the Valley. We're only a half-day's ride from Austin." She unfurled the fan and fanned her cheeks, her silver-gray gaze on him, waiting and watching for his response.

"A half-day's ride is still too far. Out of the blue, I've been offered an extraordinary opportunity. I'll not be on the trail anymore. The judge says there's a fine law school in Austin. With Judge Riordan as my mentor—Celine, he says I could have a future in politics."

Her gaze widened. "Sit behind a desk-you? I cannot imagine anything more absurd. You're a lawman through and through. Trade your six-shooters for a law book—I can't see it."

"Then I want a divorce."

Her chin dropped, her cheeks paled. "Really, Sam?" Her voice wavered. "Are you sure? Don't you remember how—" She broke off as two men entered the sitting room. She rose and said in a low tone, "Maybe we should continue our discussion upstairs...in private."

"Mrs. Foley doesn't allow female guests in male rooms."

"She'll make an *exception*," she said with some heat, her cheeks flushing. "I'm your wife, as everyone in town knows by now."

Dear God. How would he ever resist her? The glowing

skin, so soft he had to clench his fists to keep from reaching out to touch her. The soft swell of her breasts beckoned. Steeling himself to resist her considerable charms, he crossed the room, closing the distance between them. "All right. We'll talk."

He followed her out into the hall, unable to keep his gaze away from the gentle sway of her hips, accentuated by the bustle.

Careful. Don't step on the damned train.

Where did she think she was, some New York City salon?

Celine walked down the familiar hallway. Which room was his? She turned, looked over her shoulder and arched a brow. "Well?"

"Number four."

"How convenient." She smiled. "I'm right across the hall. In three."

He unlocked his door and opened it, waiting for her to enter.

"Thank you." She glided into his room, where a wide bed took up most of the space. A small writing desk was situated under the window. Much like her own room, although her bed wasn't big enough for two. "Very nice."

He pulled the chair out from the desk and motioned for her to sit. Then he took a seat on the side of the bed. "Now talk."

Already she felt the awkwardness of their situation pressing on her. He certainly wasn't going to make it easy. The bed. His nearness. Both so enticing. "Let me say, Sam, that no matter what we decide tonight, I'm prepared to return your money-most of it, anyway."

"Generous to a fault." He gave her a most insincere smile.

She folded her hands primly in her lap. "I'll say it right now. I don't want a divorce. I love you as much as I ever did. We could have a happy life together here in Kenton Valley."

"They already have a sheriff and two able deputies. I'm not needed here. My job's in Austin. I'm sure you remember that fact."

"Oh yes, and now you're going to be a lawyer. Samuel Dunaway, Esquire. Sounds mighty fine." Too fine for the likes of her.

He nodded. "Lawyering is a *mighty fine* calling. And I'll need a wife who'll support me and my new career."

"So, just like that, you've decided you're going to leave the marshals and take the judge up on his offer."

"Yeah." He loosened his string tie and unbuttoned his top shirt button. Then he toed off his boots. "It's an unexpected opportunity. One I don't intend to pass up."

Getting comfortable, wasn't he? "So you need a wife to run your household and a hostess to entertain clients and political bigwigs, a wife who isn't the daughter of a New Orleans madam. No wonder you want a divorce."

"You'll make a mighty fine wife and hostess, Celine. No one has to know about your past."

She let out an exasperated huff. "Lest you forget, Antoine Thibodaux still knows all about my past. That's why I ran in the first place. It would get around eventually. And he'll find me again, if I come with you to Austin."

"What people think doesn't matter—to me, anyway."

"Well, it matters to me!" She stood, once again ready

to run away. "You weren't sent away to school where you had to dissemble every time someone asked about your home or your parents. I hated lying."

He stood, moving between her and the door, effectively blocking her exit. "That's what you do best, isn't it? Run away. Go ahead."

He stood so close she fancied she could hear the quickening beat of his heart. Her breathing grew rapid. Breathless, she tried to stumble toward the door.

He grabbed her wrist and pulled her to his chest.

"Don't, Sam. We have to say good-bye. Now, before it hurts any worse. I'll give you your divorce. Go to Austin and become that fine lawyer. Maybe one day you'll be a judge or even the governor."

"You're not leaving. You're coming with me."

"No!" She tried to pull away, but he held her fast. "I still have three dresses to make for the Grange dance."

"To hell with the dance. Let their mamas make their dresses."

"You don't understand. I promised. And I mean to keep my promises."

"What about the ones you made to me four years ago?" His voice grew husky with emotion. "What happened to 'love, honor and obey'?"

She hung her head. "I only have trouble with that last one."

"I guess you do at that." He let out a bark of genuine laughter.

His amusement at her expense was her undoing. He could always make her laugh. Her heart raced. Damn. Her drawers had dampened with desire. If she didn't get out of here soon, her dress would be on the floor.

Sam started undoing the silk-covered buttons down the front of her ensemble.

"No, no. We can't," she cried, breathless with wanting and need. Her heart cried *yes, yes, yes*.

The top of her corset revealed, she shook her head as he bent his head to tenderly kiss the swells of flesh. "No..." she moaned. "No," she said, this time with more resolve. With all her strength, she pulled away and ran, clasping her garments together with one hand. Across the hall, only three steps to her door. She fumbled in her reticule for her key.

"That's far enough." Sam, right behind her. She opened the door and tried to keep him out, but he was too strong. He pushed in behind her, then kicked the door shut, his eyes glittering with desire as he crossed the room. A lock of his dark hair fell across his forehead, giving him a rakish look. "This would've been more comfortable in my room. Bigger bed."

"Sam..."

"You said you loved me as much as ever. Then show me how much you love me. And then we can say goodbye for good."

Tears welling in her eyes, Celine nodded. God, she wanted him so much there was no way in heaven she could resist him. He ripped off his jacket and waistcoat.

Her fingers trembled as she unbuttoned his shirt. After easing her arms from the bodice, he set it aside. He untied the skirt, allowing her to step from it.

"Undo the corset. I can't breathe," she said, gasping for air.

He untied her corset, then shucked his trousers and underwear, leaving her in the loose chemise and split-tail drawers. He thrust two fingers between her legs. "You're wet already." He picked her up, her legs automatically going around his hips. Settling her warm heat on top of his cock, not yet ready to enter her, then carried her to the bed and laid her upon it. He lifted the chemise over her head. Her nipples, already tightening into points of pleasure, brushed against the light fur of his chest.

"Now," she murmured. "I don't want to wait"

He placed a trail of nibbling kisses on her neck, each one causing swirls of need to center between her legs. Her slender hand grasped his thick cock, and she opened herself to him. She began to move, gripping him with her inner walls tighter and tighter with each quick stroke.

He imprisoned her wrists above her head with one hand and used the other to maneuver one of her breasts into his mouth. He sucked, then scraped the tender skin with his teeth.

He slowed the pace. She shook her head. "Faster."

"No. Needs to last, seeing as how this is our last time."

Was it really? Would he really leave her after the trials were over and just ride away? Could he?

The male musk of his body combined with her lavender scent. The tension grew in her belly and her core. Just when she thought she'd die if he didn't increase the pace, he did, thrusting hard and deep, harder and deeper than ever. She exploded over the cresting wave of passion, taking him with her. He groaned her name, his length pulsing within her walls.

Tears welled, threatening to spill. How could she give him up? How could she let this man ride away and never see him again? How could he leave her after what they'd shared?

The thoughts of the life they could've shared, if not for her past, sent her into a bout of sobbing.

He levered onto his elbows and gazed down at her. "What's wrong? I thought it was pretty damned great. Did I hurt you?"

"No, just go. Go on to your new life. Get out of here." Still sobbing, she pushed on his shoulder, attempting to get away from him.

He held her fast in his arms. "But, darlin', you should be a part of that life," he said tenderly. "You're not making any sense."

"I should never have come to town tonight. I thought I could make you change your mind by showing you what you were missing."

Rolling his weight off her body, he gave her a seductive smile. "You succeeded the hell out of that."

Celine scooted away from him. "But that was before the judge offered you the opportunity of a lifetime. I can't hold you back."

"It's an opportunity, but I don't have to take him up on it."

"But you want to, don't you?" Of course, he wanted to. It was plain as day just how much he did.

He hesitated, then said, "Yes, I'd like to see what could come of it."

"Then you *have* to do it."

"Not if it means losing you." He tried pulling her back into his arms, but she resisted. "No!"

"That's your last word?"

Swiping away tears, she hardened her heart. Raising her chin a notch, she said, "Yes. I want a divorce too. So go!"

His expression darkened. Jaw clenched, he stood and slowly redressed. With each garment he donned, he became more remote. Less touchable. Less tempting. Less hers.

Finally dressed, he stood at the door. "Last chance."

Averting her gaze, she clenched her jaw, resisting the compelling urge to beg him to stay.

"So be it," he said. "See you in court."

Chapter Eighteen

Amazed by Celine's composure, Sam sat in the schoolhouse-cum-courtroom, his hands clasped in front, his thumbs twiddling. A man would think she testified in court every day. Again, she'd abandoned her usual attempt to appear dowdy and plain, instead wearing a well-tailored walking suit with a high neck. The garment was light brown, trimmed in darker brown lace. And the way it emphasized her tiny waist left him a little breathless. He knew just how tiny she was even without a corset. But those memories had no place in the courtroom.

She'd already testified to the bare facts: O'Reilly had shot and killed Hunt and Fisher right before her eyes.

Now it was time for the defense, such as it was, to cross-examine her. Robert Finley, O'Reilly's lawyer, was a sandy-haired, middle-aged man accompanied by the smell of cheap whiskey, not quite covered by his bay rum cologne, wafting about his person. However, he appeared sober and steady enough when he approached the bench.

"Miz Dunaway, is it?" he began. "Would you mind stating your name again for the court? I'm a little confused since I was under the impression your name was Selma Nelson, owner of the dry-goods store."

"That's correct. My true name is Celine Boudreau

Dunaway, but around here I'm known as Selma Nelson."

Judge Riordan frowned at Celine over his eyeglasses. "You have two names?"

"Yes, Your Honor. When I left my husband several years ago, I changed my name, but my name doesn't matter. I—"

"Your Honor, please remind the witness to answer my questions and resist the urge to pontificate."

The judge raised his brows. "Mrs. Dunaway, please just answer the questions. No more. No less. And especially no pontificating." A wry grin threatened to spread into a something wider.

Sam smiled to himself. If the judge could keep Celine from running off at the mouth, more power to him.

"Sorry." She squared her shoulders. "Like I told you before, I saw Mr. O'Reilly shoot Booker Hunt and Dooley Fisher. He killed them both right in front of my eyes."

Finley hooked his thumbs in his braces and strutted forward. "Would you mind telling this court what happened to turn my client into a veritable killing machine? That's what you're describing anyways."

Instead of speaking, Celine folded her arms across her breasts. She was stalling. Why? "Mrs. Dunaway or Nelson, whatever you're called, please answer my question."

"Well... It might've had something to do with my comment about the gold."

"What gold?"

Yeah, what gold?

"Oh, there wasn't any, really. I might've intimated to the defendant that Mr. Hunt and Mr. Fisher had gold stashed away from the earlier bank robbery and sort of suggested that Mr. O'Reilly should demand his share. It was merely a ruse to distract them so I could get to the six-shooter I had hidden in my sewing basket."

"You *intimated*?" The lawyer raised his eyebrows is apparent disbelief. "Don't you mean you actually came right out and *lied*, saying Mr. Hunt and Mr. Fisher had gold stashed away and were cheating my client?"

"Well..." She glanced down at her folded hands, demonstrating a demure primness. "Yes. That's pretty much what I did."

Sonofabitch. She hadn't breathed a word about that. Pretty smart.

"So you're saying you *lied*, and as a result of those lies, two men ended up dead."

"To be truthful—" she began.

"Yes, please be truthful, Mrs. Dunaway," the judge interjected. From his sagging shoulders to his clenched jaw, Riordan appeared growing weary with Celine's testimony. Granted, she could be trying at the best of times.

"They argued a bit, then Mr. Hunt drew on Mr. O'Reilly, so he in turn drew and shot

Mr. Hunt. Then Mr. Fisher pulled his gun, but the Irishman—sorry, Mr. O'Reilly—shot Mr. Fisher right between the eyes."

At her statement, a buzz spread among the spectators.

"Silence in the court!" Riordan rapped the gavel against the desktop.

Shut up, Celine.

What was she trying to do, get O'Reilly off on a self-defense plea? Finley set his hands on his hips and strutted up to Celine. "So you're saying my client acted in self-defense?"

As if realizing what she'd done, Celine drew herself up. "No. That's not exactly—"

"Yes!" Finley got up in her face. "That's exactly what you did. You incited the deaths of two men. I say you, *not* my client, is the real killer of—"

"Oh, good grief!" Celine started to stand, then seemed to reconsider. "The Irishman is a killer. He also killed the two men the sheriff sent to guard the ranch. For heaven's sake, we're not talking about decent, law-abiding citizens. Those two men were killers. They were holding us prisoner. And by *us* I mean, the sheriff's wife, his new baby, Mrs. Crayton—they'd already shot and killed her husband—and me. They intended to bargain with our lives to get Arvil Barnes released from jail."

"*Your Honor. Please* caution the witness to answer only the questions put to her."

"First, I have to caution *you*" –the judge pointed his gavel at Finley—"from testifying and pontificating. It's obvious to everyone what happened in that house. Move on."

Finley gave a heavy sigh. "The defense rests, Your Honor."

"Mrs. Dunaway, you may step down."

Celine smiled sweetly at the judge. "Thank you, Your Honor."

With her back straight and her head held high, she walked up the aisle, swishing past Sam, so close he could smell the lavender fragrance he'd grown to associate with her presence.

"We'll stop for dinner, then we'll have closing arguments, and the jury can deliberate with full stomachs." The judge smacked the gavel on the desktop.

Wouldn't be long now, Sam mused, marveling at the idea he might wield such power one day.

Still, he had a duty to perform. He rose, cuffed the prisoner and returned him to his cell. He'd catch up with his beautiful wife later. Damn the woman. Was a career in law worth giving up the woman he loved? Her testimony had more than proved her value. Here was a woman who'd been able to turn three desperate outlaws against each other. Then she'd been smart and brave enough to lead the worst of the lot away from the sheriff's family, risking her very own life.

Sure, she'd run off and damn near broken his heart, but again, she'd done it to protect him from scandal. She'd made a new, even respectable, life for herself. He allowed himself a wry grin. Seemed like a small matter now that she'd stolen his money to do it. Life didn't offer many second chances. He'd be a fool to pass on this one.

After leaving the trial, Celine walked straight to her store. It seemed like forever since she'd closed it to help Star with the baby's layette. Now that baby was in his mama's arms and the layette complete, even if part of it was finished after he was born.

Nearing the store, she spied little Billy Rasmussen. He ran to meet her with a big smile. "Miss Nelson, ya sure do look purty today. Did ya go to the trial? Are they gonna hang 'im?" "Thank you, Billy. Yes, I was at the trial, but I don't know the outcome as it's not over yet."

"Where ya been? I wanted some peppermint, but my ma said the store was closed and I'd have to wait"

She smiled down at the rambunctious boy. "I'm

opening the store right now, and you shall have your peppermint. Maybe even two, since I've been away."

"What were ya doin'?"

"I was helping out at the sheriff's ranch."

"Heard my ma say they got a new baby. Reckon they might let me play with 'im?"

Celine unlocked the door and walked inside. She'd have to dust, but first, candy for an inquisitive little boy. "The baby is pretty tiny. It'll be a while before he's big and strong enough to play with a young man like you."

He puffed out his chest. "Yeah, reckon so. I'm purty strong, all right. Did I tell ya I was goin' to be a lawman?"

"That's wonderful, Billy." At least the child was thinking ahead. He'd soon have a real-life example for what happened to boys who grew up to be outlaws.

"That marshal fella said I'd have to mind my ma and study. Reckon I can do that?"

"I'm sure of it" She opened the peppermint jar and selected two candies for the youngster. "Here you go."

He popped one in his mouth and jammed the other into his breeches pocket, then waved. "Bye!"

She smiled. His joy in life was infectious. Then, remembering that soon she'd be a divorced woman with no chance of a family or a delightful child like the one who'd just left, she felt her joy dim and let out a sigh.

She spent the next few minutes dusting the counter and shelves. When that onerous task was completed, she headed back to the sewing room. Three dresses to complete in very little time.

Putting the major pieces together hadn't taken much effort, but the special embellishments her clients loved were much more time-consuming. And they all had to be different. The dresses would be ready for a first fitting by the end of the week. The girls' dress forms took up quite a bit of room, but having the forms close at hand reduced the number of adjustments needed for the perfect fit she was known for. Two of the girls were slender as reeds and would need ruffles over the bodice, while the third young woman was plumper. Still, she'd have a beautiful dress for the Grange dance.

Time passed quickly while she focused on the work at hand; she didn't hear the door open until the bell over the door jangled. Startled, she looked up. "Be right there."

She saw the silhouette of a man standing in her shop. Sam. She'd know his broad-shouldered, lean-hipped form anywhere.

"What now?" she asked, making no attempt to moderate the exasperation in her tone.

Removing his Stetson and setting it on the counter, he leveled his gaze on her. "The jury returned from dinner, deliberated a quarter of an hour and found O'Reilly guilty of the five murders. My job's done. The judge is taking the morning stage, and I'll be riding back to Austin."

"Have a safe trip." He was about to leave, and she'd never see him again. Her eyes stung with unshed tears. Unable to say more, she clenched her jaw to keep her bottom lip from trembling.

"I just wanted to say good-bye. I'll have my attorney contact yours. I assume you have one?"

She swallowed the lump in her throat. "You saw him in court today."

"Finley?" Sam shook his head.

"This town isn't big enough to support two lawyers," she said wryly.

"Guess not."

"One more thing." She moved behind the counter, pulled out her checkbook, dipped her pen into the inkwell, wrote the check and carefully tore it out. "This will cover eighty percent of of what I took."

He took the check and glanced at it, eyebrows raised.

"I'll pay you the balance within six months...with interest, of course. Is my word good enough, or shall I call Mr. Finley to draw up a quick agreement?"

He folded the check in half and slid it inside a jacket pocket. "Your word is sufficient. I wish you'd reconsider and come with me."

"I've already made a life here, Sam. And I'm busy." She shot a quick glance at the door to her sewing room.

A smirk played about his lips. "Yeah, three dresses to sew before the Grange dance."

"Exactly."

"I'll be going, then."

The heated expression in his eyes sent shivers up her spine. His mouth twitched. Was he going to kiss her?

Guess not.

Instead of prolonging the goodbye, he strode to the door. All she could do was watch him walk across the rutted main street to the sheriff's office...and out of her life forever.

She swallowed the lump in her throat. It was better this way. He could still find a wife and have children. A wife who wouldn't embarrass him.

She picked up a dust cloth and dusted the counter a second time. If only she could rid her past of the dirt, or at least the dirt that ordinary folks would assign her.

Stop feeling sorry for yourself. You have work to do.

A tear streaked its way down her cheek. No, she'd have to wait until her tears were dried. Wouldn't do to get tear stains on any of the silk fabrics.

Chapter Nineteen

The week after Sam left for Austin passed in a blur. It seemed as if every woman in town required something from the dry-goods store. More likely they wanted to have a look at the spinster seamstress who turned out to be married to the marshal. In between ringing up sales, she'd worked hard on the three dresses. Yes, she'd focused on sewing and worked even harder to forget Sam Dunaway had ever come back into her life, however briefly. But at night, the loneliness nearly overwhelmed her, no matter how many hours she spent sewing. Every single night, she cried herself to sleep, unable to forget the intensity of their lovemaking.

Two of the dresses were already completed and delivered. This one would only need a minor adjustment. She pinned a tiny tuck into the back of the bodice. "There that should do it, Becky."

The young woman reached around to check the fit, then beamed. "You're wonderful. I swear we're so lucky to have a dressmaker with your skills here in town." She gave a squeal and spun around.

"I'm happy if you're happy, dear." Celine, who was feeling more and more like the old Selma, restrained a sigh.

Becky gazed into the mirror, admiring herself, then turned to face Celine. "You're coming to the dance, aren't you? What are you wearing? Something splendid, I'm sure."

Celine shook her head. "I hadn't planned on attending. Dances aren't for old women like me."

"Oh, go on. You're not that old. My mother's going, and you're not nearly as old as she is."

"I'm sure your mother wouldn't appreciate hearing sentiments like that." Celine shrugged. "Well...perhaps I will go and watch you dance. Or serve lemonade."

The young woman cocked her head to the side. "I heard you're actually married to that handsome marshal who was in town last week."

"I am...for now."

"Is he coming back for the dance?"

"No." Time to nip this conversation in the bud. "I'm really not comfortable discussing my private life."

Becky's cheeks flushed and her pink lips formed an O, but she recovered quickly. "Anyway, I hope to see you. I know my dress is the prettiest. Confess, you like it the best of all, don't you?" She twirled around, then curtseyed to an imaginary dance partner.

"I don't play favorites with my dresses. I make each one to suit the wearer. Each of your dresses is as lovely as I can make them. I've seen to that."

Being careful of the pins, Becky quickly removed her new dress and changed into her every-day gingham.

Celine let out a loud sigh. To be so young and carefree...

Before the door could shut behind Becky, young Billy Rasmussen breezed through it into the shop. He stopped, removed his billed cap and offered her a bow. "I've come to see if I could escort ya to the dance, Miss Nelson."

Celine smiled down at the boy. "I appreciate the offer, Billy. Perhaps you should squire your ma. I'll save a dance for you, though." Admittedly, her dance card was nonexistent.

"Will ya?" The boy jumped a foot. "Wowee!" He spun and ran from the store.

Now that she'd committed to going to the dance, what would she wear? Something dignified. No point in attracting attention. Oh dear, with every passing day since Sam had left, it seemed as if she was in grave danger of becoming Selma again. Only Sam could make her feel like Celine.

She headed back to her sewing room to complete the last adjustment on Becky's dress when the bell over the door jangled again. She turned to see Starlight Tate carrying her newborn son.

"Star! What are you doing in town?" Celine held out her hands. "Let me see that baby. I can't believe it. He's grown so much." She rocked the baby in her arms. Oh, that new-baby smell.

"I'm in desperate need of something to wear to the Grange dance. I'm afraid I'm a couple of inches from getting into my best dress."

"But the dance is tomorrow night!"

Star clasped her hands in front as if praying or begging. "Oh please, I don't need anything fancy. Just *new*. I may be an old married lady with a baby, but I don't want to look like one. It'll need to have a front opening so I can leave to nurse the baby. Mainly, I'll just sit on the side with the other matrons. And maybe, just maybe, I'll dance the last waltz with my husband."

Infected by her friend's energy, Celine could hardly wait to start on a new dress. "Then, I'd better get busy," she said, handing the infant back to his mother. "I'll have to work all night, but I'm happy to make your new dress."

Quickly, Star chose the fabric, buttons and trim.

Celine gathered up the purchases and took them back to the sewing room. She returned with a smile. "The last time I had to work this fast was for your wedding. You really should learn to give your favorite dressmaker a little more leeway."

"I know. I'm impulsive. Cord said it was too soon for me to be out and going to a dance, so I decided I was going. Simple as that."

"And you hate to be told you can't do something."

"Right you are. You know me too well. Doesn't she, Carlos?" She leaned down and kissed the baby's forehead. Emerald eyes sparkling, she glanced back at Celine. "Now then, what are you wearing?"

"I haven't given it much thought. It won't be new-that's for sure." Celine smiled. "You went ahead and named him Carlos."

"Yes, but don't tell Cord. He thought he came up with the idea for the baby's name."

"You're incorrigible!"

"Just part of my redheaded charm."

After taking Star's measurements and noting the differences on the shop's dress form, Celine stopped, setting her hands on her hips. "Go see your husband or something. I've got work to do."

Star adjusted the baby's clothes. "And now what'll you wear?"

"Doesn't matter what I wear. Shoo!" she said. "Go on!"

"But it does. Don't you want to look as pretty as all your creations?"

"I'll pull something out. Don't worry. I've a lot of dresses I haven't worn since I've been in the Valley."

"Really? I want to see."

"I don't have time-unless you want to show up with your dress half-done?"

All right! I'm going. What time shall I pick it up?"

Celine worried her bottom lip between her teeth. "I'll send it home with your husband in time to get ready for the dance, okay?"

"Okay!" Star maneuvered the baby into a better carrying position. "Honestly, you're such a grouch since Sam left."

"Do *not* mention his name. He's gone. End of story." She made a shooing motion with her hands. "Go!"

"I'm gone!"

Celine let out a sigh as soon as the door closed behind her friend. If Celine never heard Sam Dunaway's name again, it would be too soon.

All night she worked on the green-and-cream-striped silk. She located a pattern with a front-opening placket, which would make it perfect for Star to nurse little Carlos. Then she unearthed a dark green silk remnant from her stores and used it to add a faux vest to the bodice as well as a wide bottom hem.

Sometime around daybreak, she tied off the last thread and cut it, completing the insertion of the second mutton-leg sleeve. She removed her thimble and set it aside on the table. Stretching her neck and shoulders, she let out a sigh.

Done.

With only a couple of hours until the dance, Celine stood in front of her chifforobe wondering who would appear that night: Selma or Celine? The spring dance wasn't anything like the formal balls held in New Orleans or back east. In Kenton Valley, the young women would still want to wear their finest and newest dresses, but mature women, married women like herself, would attend the dance wearing anything from gingham checks to silk, sometimes years out of fashion.

She chose a bronze silk dress with mutton-leg sleeves and a small bustle. The neck was high with a band of lace. The bodice had a scooped yoke with a row of pearl buttons and tiny tucks on each side of the buttons.

The dress's silken sheen seemed to make her skin glow. Dangling earrings of amber and gold completed the ensemble she'd designed and sewn two years earlier. As soon as the silk had arrived, she hadn't been able to resist setting it aside. And as she'd had no real occasion to wear it, no one had ever seen it.

Frankly, other than her promise to save Billy Rasmussen a dance, there was still no real reason for her to attend this event. On the other hand, she really looked forward to seeing the three young women arrayed in all their finery.

With a wry smile, she thought the House of Worth need not worry. Her humble gowns, while lovely, were no competition.

She entered the Grange Hall. A table with

refreshments sat on her immediate right. The musicians were positioned at the far end of the hall on the dais, while rows of chairs lined both sides of the hall. The dancing had already begun, a lively reel. Unable to resist, her toes tapped to the rhythm. How she'd missed dancing, but she held back the impulse to totally embarrass herself by whirling around the dance floor.

Spying Star sitting on the right with other young matrons, Celine waved. Star waved furiously, gesturing for Celine to come over. Star's dress fit beautifully and showed her slightly fuller figure to perfection. If not for the babe in her arms, no one would ever know she'd recently given birth.

"It's been so long since I attended a Grange dance," Star said. "This time last year, I was still in Boston with my ma."

Celine sat beside her friend and leaned forward. "Does she know about Carlos?"

Star rolled her eyes. "Yes. I had Cord send her a telegram, but I've not heard anything back. Not even so much as a congratulations." Star shrugged. "Doesn't matter."

"I'm sorry."

"I didn't expect anything-not really. Besides, I have all the family I need. Cord, Carlos, and the rest of Cord's family—they treat me like royalty. My pa has even quit his drinking."

Celine straightened and glanced around the hall. "Where is he?"

"He's escorting Widow Loomis tonight. They should be here any minute."

"Really. At his age?"

"Just goes to show you never know." Star giggled. "I may have a stepmother soon."

The music changed from a reel to a waltz. And before Celine could respond to Star's stepmother remark, Billy Rasmussen skidded to a stop in front of her and bowed. "Ya save a dance for me?" he asked with a huge smile that showed his dimples.

"Do you know how to waltz?"

"No, ma'am." He looked over his shoulder at the dancers. "But it don't look too hard."

Celine smiled. "It isn't." She rose, holding out her hand. "Now, if you'll stand beside me, we'll do the steps side by side. Once you have them down, we'll face each other."

"All right!" The boy pulled her forward onto the dance floor.

The boy was a quick learner. In fact, he had a natural grace about him. "Let's switch now," she suggested. "I think you know what you're doing."

She faced him, and he smiled up, his bright blue eyes shining with excitement.

So intent was she on her young partner and keeping them from bumping into the other couples that the sound of a deep male voice startled her. "May I cut in, Master Rasmussen?"

"Marshal, yes, sir! I wouldn't let just anybody dance with Miss Nelson."

"Most appreciated, young sir."

Celine's breath caught in her throat as the boy ran off to join his friends. "Sam, what are you doing here?" He'd even worn the very suit she'd made him before she'd run away. Black, still perfectly tailored to his lean muscular form. A black waistcoat and a wine-colored silk cravat. And so handsome her heart nearly stopped. "I thought—"

He swept her into his strong arms, and they began gliding over the floor in the waltz's familiar rhythm. Oh God, this felt so right.

"I have a plan—if you'll hear me out." His gaze was warm as he led her around the floor, his movements easy and surprisingly graceful.

A plan? "It's wonderful to see you," she began, still stunned that he'd actually come to the dance, "but I thought we had this all settled and done."

"Maybe *you* did, but I don't give up that easily. You should know that by now." He smiled down at her, his gaze warm and inviting.

How could she be expected to keep her head with him so close? But she gave it her best effort. "I know exactly how stubborn you are."

"But will you hear me out?"

He pulled her closer, making it easier for her to lose herself in the waltz...and more difficult to keep her mind on their conversation. "What's the point? We're at an impasse. We can't both have what we want—no, what we need."

"What if I purchased a piece of land halfway between Austin and here? That would make it a quarter-day's ride to either Austin or the Valley."

"That's still too far," she said with a regretful shake of her head. "Two hours is still a long ride every day, twice a day. I have a shop that needs to open first thing each morning." He spun her under his arm. "Well, suppose I bought you a shop in Austin? You could do a thriving business. And once word got around about your nimble fingers, you'd have all the clientele you could handle."

"But what about you?" God, was the room spinning, or was it her head? "What will *you* do?"

"Judge Riordan has officially taken me on as his clerk. I'll study law at the university—he's already recommended me to one of the law professors."

"Already?" So many changes. So much to consider. "I never thought about opening a shop in Austin." Without missing a step, she asked, "What about my shop here?"

"You could sell it or hire someone you trust to run it for you."

"Two shops?" Intriguing idea. "If you buy the shop, where would we live?"

"Depends on the location. We could live above the shop or rent a small house on the outskirts of town."

"I don't know, Sam."

"What do you say, Celine? Be my wife again. Come with me to Austin."

"I'll give it some thought." *Give it some thought? Yes, yes, yes.*

"Think fast, then." He stopped dancing and pulled her to the side. "I have a confession to make."

"What now?" She took a deep breath, holding back a groan. The man was so unpredictable. Heaven only knew what he was about to say.

"I've already bought the shop. It's about the same size as the one here, and there's plenty of space for living quarters above the store."

"You've already *bought* it?" She stepped back. "You're pretty sure of yourself, Marshal Dunaway."

"I'm *sure* I can't live without you."

"But the cost..."

"I used the money you paid me—the money I'd saved for *our* future. What was the point in saving it if I couldn't have you with me?"

Her heart raced. Could it be? Could they really be together the way she wanted? Could she have him and her shop too? Yes. Yes, she could. "Oh, Sam, I love you." She flung her arms around his neck.

"I love you too, darlin'. And don't forget it." He spun her around, her heart reeling and bursting with love.

"But my past—"

"If anyone dares mention your past, I'll sue 'em."

Her lips parted, pulling into a smile. "All right."

"So you'll come to Austin? I need to hear you say it again, out loud."

"Just try keeping me away."

He clutched her to his chest, kissing her until all she could think about was a real marriage, a home and a family.

And best of all... Sam, the man the man at her side, the man she would love forever and ever.

And never ever run from again.

The End

Bonus Material

Continue enjoying the lawman saga with stories about Kenton Valley's modern day lawmen and their loves.

Hunted

Hill Country Lawmen 1
Marie-Nicole Ryan
Available now

"They found two bodies, Sheriff," Dorothy, the dispatcher, said. "Your ranch...out by Simon's Creek."

"Who called it in?" Vince asked.

"Damn inconsiderate so-and-so hung up." She let out a loud huff over the phone. "Didn't leave his name."

"All right. Thanks." Sheriff Vince Tate punched the button, terminating the call. Now which of his ranch hands had made the call and upset the elderly dispatcher with his rudeness? No point in that.

Simon's Creek was a dry bed that wound through most of Los Marcos County, including the northern edge of the Tate ranch. Not the first time a flash flood had unearthed ancient remains. Better put in a call to the state archeologist, Abe Duckworth, who handled these cases.

Vince called Duckworth, giving him the details and location. "Meet you there." He disconnected the call, then headed to the outer office. Nodding at Dorothy, he stopped. "You know where I'm headed. Shouldn't be long."

"Want me to notify Will, Sheriff?" She nodded, never once disturbing her tightly wound gray curls. "He's responding to a fender bender on Highway 18."

Vince shook his head. His chief deputy, Will Rasmussen, handled forensics. "Doubt we'll need him.

Probably native remains."

"Drive safe then."

"Always." Setting his Stetson on his head, he hid the smile threatening to break through. The dispatcher never failed to add her "Drive safe" warning when one of them left the office. A widow, she treated him and his deputies like the sons and daughters she never had. Not a bad way to start the day.

He stepped outside. The Texas sun beat down like Hell on steroids. Only May, but if today's temperature was an indicator, a blistering summer was already here. His Chevy Tahoe sat in the parking lot, waves of heat rising from the hood.

Welcome to Texas. Still, he wouldn't trade living here for any other state or country on earth. He opened the door, stepped back to evade the escape of super-heated air. He climbed inside, the seats still blistering hot through his jeans, and set his hat on the seat.

His com unit squawked. He grabbed the mic and nearly dropped the scorching plastic instrument. "Yeah?" he answered.

"It's Will. I'm over at your place."

"Thought you were working an MVA?"

"Finished. Didn't amount to much anyway. I was close so I thought I might as well..."

"I've already called Abe."

"Up to you, of course. These remains don't appear that old."

Not what he wanted to hear. "Okay. On my way." He reversed from his parking spot, flipped on his lights and siren, then headed down Main Street. He passed the drugstore, and his mind went automatically to pharmacist

Abby Fields.

Yes, Abby Fields with silky dark, almost black hair.

And dancing green eyes.

A warm and willing body.

The only woman he'd ever loved.

Why couldn't she have just stayed the hell in Atlanta.

Her sudden decision to go to school at the University of Georgia in Athens, instead of UT in Austin as they'd planned—the final break in their relationship.

Was he supposed to forgive her for trashing their relationship after he'd left for college? No way!

Her father's murder six months ago brought her back to Kenton Valley. Oh hell, welcome to heartache round two. Still, he'd managed to remain professional and arrest her father's killer to boot.

After that, she really should've gone back to Atlanta. But no, she'd moved back and run her father's drugstore. Forever a daily reminder of her deception.

On top of everything else, he still couldn't find his runaway wife. If divorce papers couldn't be served, how the hell could he divorce her?

Dammit! He clenched his jaw. Jammed the Tahoe into fourth gear and headed east to Simon's Creek.

About the Author

Marie-Nicole Ryan was born in a small western Kentucky town, but after college and marriage, she said "Good-bye" to small town life. After spending three years as an army wife, she landed in Nashville, TN, where she spent several decades working as an RN and case manager. Finally in 2002, she achieved her dream of becoming a published author.

She loves writing about lawmen and detectives and writes erotic historical western romance and contemporary romantic suspense. *Too Good to be True* won a 2008 EPPIE for erotic romantic suspense. One of her early books, *See You in My Dreams*, won the Golden Wings award from the publisher for excellence in romantic suspense. In addition, her mystery/ suspense novel, *One Too Many*, was a 2009 EPPIE Finalist.

A former active member of RWA® and Music City Romance Writers, she recently returned to her old hometown in western Kentucky. When she's not slaving away at her current work in progress, you might find her walking her dog, Kelsea, a Sheltie rescue, or at the Y. But you won't ever find her in an airplane. No, not ever.

Web site: https://www.marienicoleryan.com
Facebook: https://facebook.com/MarieNicoleRyan.author
Twitter: http://www.twitter.com/marienicoleryan
email: marie@marienicoleryan.com